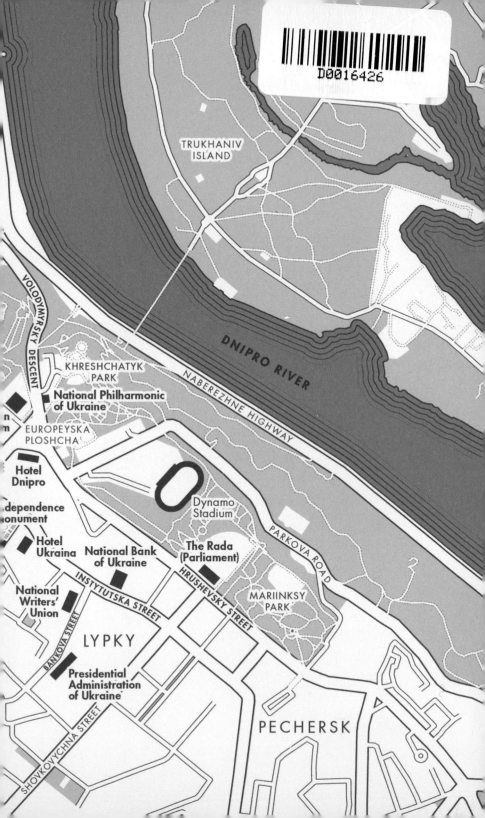

TRUKHANIV
ISLAND

DNIPRO RIVER

NABEREZHNE HIGHWAY

KHRESHCHATYK
PARK

National Philharmonic
of Ukraine

n
m

EUROPEYSKA
PLOSHCHA

Hotel
Dnipro

dependence
onument

Hotel
Ukraina

National Bank
of Ukraine

Dynamo
Stadium

The Rada
(Parliament)

PARKOVA ROAD

INSTYTUTSKA STREET

HRUSHEVSKY STREET

MARIINKSY
PARK

National
Writers'
Union

BANKOVA STREET

LYPKY

Presidential
Administration
of Ukraine

SHOVKOVYCHNA STREET

PECHERSK

VOLODYMYRSKY DESCENT

INDEPENDENCE
SQUARE

Also by A. D. Miller

Snowdrops
The Earl of Petticoat Lane
The Faithful Couple

INDEPENDENCE SQUARE

A. D. Miller

Harvill *Secker*
LONDON

1 3 5 7 9 10 8 6 4 2

Harvill Secker, an imprint of Vintage,
20 Vauxhall Bridge Road,
London SW1V 2SA

Harvill Secker is part of the Penguin Random House group of companies
whose addresses can be found at global.penguinrandomhouse.com

Penguin
Random House
UK

First published by Harvill Secker in 2020

A CIP catalogue record for this book is available from the British Library

penguin.co.uk/vintage

ISBN 9781787301788 (hardback)
ISBN 9781787301795 (trade paperback)

Typeset in 10.75/15.75 pt Scala-Regular
by Integra Software Services Pvt. Ltd, Pondicherry

Printed and bound in Great Britain by Clays Ltd, Elcograf S.p.A.

The lyrics remembered by Simon in Chapter viii come from the song 'Если у
вас нету тёти', written by Alexander Aronov and performed by Sergey Nikitin.

The lyrics quoted in Chapter 4 are from the Jefferson Airplane song
'Somebody to Love' written by Darby R. Slick.

Penguin Random House is committed to a sustainable future for
our business, our readers and our planet. This book is made from
Forest Stewardship Council® certified paper.

MIX
Paper from
responsible sources
FSC® C018179

For Milly and Jacob
And for my mother Amelia

There are decades where nothing happens; and there are weeks where decades happen.

Attributed to Vladimir Lenin

Author's note – and a brief history of a revolution

For its backdrop, this book reimagines the Orange Revolution, which took place in Kiev in the winter of 2004–5, and its sad aftermath. But its main characters – including the Ukrainians and the British diplomats – are all invented, as is the story and its fictional climax on the night of 1 December. Any resemblance to actual living individuals is coincidental, not intended and should not be inferred. The actions of real-life figures involved in the events (see below) have been fictionalised in the novel, too. The revolution was dramatically public yet also, at crucial moments, opaque; in part *Independence Square* unfolds in the resulting gaps.

These, in brief, are the real events that took place within the time-frame of the novel:

September 2004: Thirteen years after the Soviet Union collapsed and Ukraine became independent, it faces a presidential election. The opposition candidate, Viktor Yushchenko, pledges to reorient his country away from neighbouring Russia and towards the West, and to fight corruption. Two months before the vote, he is mysteriously poisoned and disfigured.

November 2004: Authorities say that Viktor Yanukovych, the candidate preferred by the old regime – and by Vladimir Putin – has won the election. Amid accusations of ballot-stuffing, protesters occupy Independence Square, led by Yushchenko, Yulia Tymoshenko – a firebrand politician – and Petro Poroshenko, a chocolate magnate.

December 2004: After violent repression is averted, the Supreme Court annuls the election result and orders a rerun. Yushchenko prevails.

February 2010: Years of infighting and allegations of corruption discredit the Orange revolutionaries; Yanukovych wins the presidency at the second attempt.

November 2013—Spring 2014: Yanukovych's ties to the Kremlin help incite new protests, which culminate in the killing of a hundred people around Independence Square. Yanukovych flees to Russia; Putin annexes Crimea and foments a war in eastern Ukraine. Thousands die.

May 2014: Amid the fighting, Poroshenko defeats Tymoshenko to be elected president.

1. Poison

SIMON tramped on the spot to keep warm, one hand grasping the pedestal of the Lenin statue for balance. He flexed his fingers in his leather gloves.

'There he is,' Jacqui said.

Her breath clouded in the winter air. From the direction of Independence Square came a low defiant rumble.

'I said, he's coming. Simon? He's here.'

He swivelled on the slick paving stone and followed her gaze. A posse of men were muscling towards them on Shevchenko Boulevard at speed. Kovrin was out in front, almost a head shorter than his entourage, swinging his arms like a child imitating a soldier. He began to talk before he came to a halt.

'Simon, so sorry. Absolutely sorry for time.' Kovrin blew out his cheeks. 'From my point of view, this is bullshit. To close all streets. Simply bullshit.'

'Don't mention it, Mr Kovrin,' Simon said. 'We're just pleased you were able to get here.'

'Misha, please. Call me Misha.' Silently, the bodyguards arced around him. 'To help my British friends? Absolutely.'

'Very kind of you,' Simon said. 'Though we hope this will be useful for you too.' Beside him, Jacqui cleared her throat. 'If I may, this is Jacqui Drayton, our public affairs officer.'

'Terrific to meet you,' Jacqui said. Her glasses had steamed up.

'Hello, my dear,' Kovrin said. 'Misha Kovrin.' He clasped her fingers and bowed, but his eyes, when he raised them, were focused on the stream of people gushing around the statue and turning towards the square. Jacqui polished her glasses.

'So many,' Kovrin murmured. 'I did not think there would be so many. Like some army.'

'Indeed,' Simon said. 'But very peaceful. Entirely. Our security officer came down earlier, he doesn't anticipate any trouble. And we can be at the embassy in five minutes if we have to be.'

Kovrin smiled. 'The embassy, yes.' He pinned back his shoulders. 'I am not Hollywood hero, but – okay! Forwards!'

At the bottom of the boulevard they turned onto Khreshchatyk, the main downtown thoroughfare. In the days since the presidential election a canvas settlement had risen on the road, the opposition's tents stretching from the square to the statue and the Besarabsky market. The denuded chestnut trees on the pavements seemed charred by the winter. Kovrin tucked in his stubbly chin and thrust his hands into the pockets of his ski jacket, elbows protruding at his sides. A woollen hat was pulled low on his brow. His camouflage only made him more conspicuous, like a burglar in a picture book.

'Yesterday, at German ambassador's reception,' Kovrin said, 'when you suggest your concept, how you will show to me the opposition, you say there is someone special to see.'

'There is. A group of young activists, my colleague met them in Lviv.' Simon glanced towards Jacqui but she was stranded behind the bodyguards. 'We think it's important for someone from your side ... It's important for you to be here.'

'No side,' Kovrin said, surveying the sea of peaked caps and technicolour flags. 'We have no side, only our country. National interest.'

'Of course,' Simon said, panting at Kovrin's pace. 'I only meant to say, we know you have some influence with the government – the television stations, your friends.'

'Private citizen. We have some friends, but absolutely private.'

'Well,' Simon said, 'we thought if you came down and saw for yourself – the people here, the atmosphere – you could explain to your friends, explain to the old president, that there's no call for any rash moves. All we want is a peaceful resolution.'

'All you want,' Kovrin said. 'It's clear.'

Smoke from the field kitchens spiralled into the gravid evening sky. Through the archways between the mansion blocks, ordinary life glinted in the neon arcades. As they approached Independence Square, the band on the stage struck up the protesters' anthem, the bassline echoing between the granite edifices built by German POWs after the war. The crowd chanted the chorus:

Together we are many!
We will not be defeated!

Three old men in sheepskin coats stood, arms linked, at the edge of the square, Red Army *ushankas* on their heads, medals on their chests. There were so many people, too many people, and newcomers who had made it past the roadblocks on the outskirts of the city were still flooding in from the side streets and along Khreshchatyk. A girl with orange bows in her pigtails sat on her father's shoulders, waving the national flag.

'Over there,' Jacqui said, indicating a banner that read *Ivano-Frankivsk Is For The Future!* 'That's them.'

The singer extended his microphone towards the crowd. *Together we are many!*

'Ah yes,' Simon said. 'This is who Jacqui ... who we'd like you to meet. Shall we go around?'

'Is okay,' Kovrin said. 'We go through.'

Straight away he collided with the father of the orange-bowed girl. The man staggered, his daughter overbalanced, yelping and dropping her flag as she reached down to break her fall. The bodyguards domed their arms above Kovrin's head; Simon stepped forward to steady the child. The father began to remonstrate, changing his mind when he noticed the guards.

'Okay,' Kovrin said. 'Forwards!'

He burrowed into the mass; from above, their group resembled a legion of cells invading a softly hospitable organism. They reached the bottom of the independence monument in the middle of the square, the golden statue of the goddess shimmering above them on her marble column. The air smelled of damp clothes and diesel fumes.

'This will do,' Simon said. 'Jacqui will fetch them for us.'

'Right,' Jacqui said. 'I suppose I will.' She pressed her glasses against her nose, took a breath like a diver going under, and disappeared into the crowd.

*

4

On the stage, the musicians yielded to the opposition candidate, his horror-movie face still disfigured from the poisoning during the election campaign. 'Dear friends,' he began, 'today our opponent declared victory.'

Shame!

'They broke up our rallies. They set fire to our offices. This, they call victory!'

'Simply bullshit!' Kovrin stage-whispered.

'They stole our votes. But they cannot steal our country!'

'Good consultants,' Kovrin said. 'Good speechwriter.'

'We refuse to be governed by thieves!'

'Means me,' Kovrin said. Simon gave an awkward chuckle.

Jacqui returned with a woman wearing mittens and a thin dark coat. The bodyguards made way for them.

'May I introduce Olesya Zarchenko?' Jacqui said. 'That's her brother over there.' She indicated a young man in a leather coat, waving an orange flag on the steps of the monument. 'She is a member of a group call—'

'Delighted,' Kovrin said, extending his hand.

Olesya's eyes widened as they confirmed what Jacqui had told her. The man said to be godfather to the outgoing president's grandson, the proprietor of two television channels, a billionaire, was here on the square, talking to her. Power's avatar, power itself, talking to Olesya Zarchenko, aged twenty-three, from Ivano-Frankivsk.

'Me also,' she said in English. Her eyes were dark-ringed, her nose reddened by the cold, but otherwise her face was pale. Kovrin grinned.

'And this is my colleague—'

'Simon Davey, from the embassy. Deputy head of mission. How do you do?'

5

'No more orders from Moscow!' said the speaker on the stage. 'No more Kremlin lies!'

'My British friends,' Kovrin said, raising his voice above the speech, 'say you can help me to understand – all this anger, these people, why you are all here.'

'Bandits out!' exclaimed the politician.

Bandits out! answered the crowd. Thousands of candles were held aloft as if for a sacrament, consecrated by a gentle snow. The votes would be counted, the universe seemed to be promising, the assassins would repent. Everyone would be different, shucking off their old, indentured pasts.

'It's clear, I think.' Olesya swallowed. 'We want to live in a free country. A normal country. Nothing more.'

'Is my country also,' Kovrin said. 'And frankly speaking, this is not normal. To take over city with your tents – this is chaos.'

'In my opinion,' Olesya said, 'it's chaos in our government. It's chaos in our police.'

'They think they can buy this election!' the disfigured candidate growled. On the giant screen beside the stage, his likeness raised a fist. 'But we are not for sale!'

Shame!

From his perch on the monument, Olesya's brother joined in: 'Shame!' She beckoned for him to join them but he didn't see her.

'Buy or no buy, he loses,' Kovrin said. 'He lost.'

'But we say no,' Olesya said. 'We didn't lose. And we will stay until we win.'

'Dear friends,' the politician cooed. 'Glory to you all!'

Glory! affirmed the square, swelling on that word as if the organism had drawn breath. The pocket of space at the foot of the monument closed, grinding Kovrin and the diplomats together. Then the organism exhaled and the space expanded again.

One of the bodyguards bent down and whispered to his boss. He rocked back on his heels and glanced around: Kovrin against the square, or against the world – he seemed content to take those odds.

'So,' he said, 'I would like to continue. There is something more to say. Mr Davey will come too, I think. At my house? Tomorrow?'

Olesya turned to Simon; he nodded. 'And my brother?' She pinned her hair behind her ear.

'Absolutely,' Kovrin said.

'Right,' Jacqui said. 'Terrific.'

'Until tomorrow,' Kovrin said to Olesya. 'I send my man with our car.'

Half a dozen other politicians joined the speaker onstage, waving and linking arms for the national anthem. The big screen broadcast wide-angle images of the crowd, letting the protesters see their own strength, the narcotic spectacle of their numberless best selves. The bodyguards led Kovrin and the diplomats towards the colonnade of the post office building, now occupied by vendors of revolutionary merchandise.

'You know,' Kovrin said, 'television news says this is all monsters. My channels, they say these are terrorists. But – off records? – to me, they look like normal people. Young. Absolutely normal.'

'Precisely,' Simon said. 'That is precisely why we wanted you to come.'

'From my point of view,' Kovrin said, pausing at a display of orange scarves, 'nothing is possible without compromise. This is my number-one point.'

'We're all in agreement there,' Simon said. Kovrin rubbed a scarf between his fingers as if assessing the fabric. 'I mean, the international community.'

'International community,' Kovrin repeated. 'You come tomorrow, yes? Is important. Good night, Miss Jenny.'

Jacqui nodded. Kovrin and his bodyguards marched away towards the opera house.

Two state security agents were keeping watch behind the stage, their cover blown by their blank expressions and the wires of their earpieces. On Mykhailivska Street, halfway up the hill that led from Independence Square to the embassy, Simon and Jacqui passed a parked bus with its engine running, its round, cartoonish headlights dimmed, curtains drawn across its windows. A group of tessellated riot policemen were smoking on the pavement, their shields stacked against the vehicle's wheels, truncheons at their hips, waiting for their orders.

The white and blue bell tower of St. Michael's monastery beckoned from the crest of the hill. Snow pirouetted in the cones of yellow cast by the street lamps, like ballerinas in their spotlights. The diplomats paused to see the fireworks that were bursting over the square. Between the bangs, the lyrics reached them as whispers:

Together we are many!
We will not be defeated!

The sound of a country going all in against itself.

'She seemed to go down well,' Jacqui said. 'Let's hope he leans on his government pals to play nicely.'

8

'Itching to crack a few skulls, some of them,' Simon said. 'But that's the idea. Clever of us to find her.'

'Right,' Jacqui said. 'Us.'

'Better sense tomorrow, I expect.' Snowflakes speckled his beard. 'Rather pretty, I have to say.'

She coughed; he half turned towards her. 'The fireworks, I mean.'

'Right,' Jacqui said. 'The fireworks.'

i. The rat

22 **August 2017**
2.04 **p.m.**

SHE DOES not see me but I see her. She is coming down the
steps in front of the Natural History Museum, near where they
set up the ice rink in the winter, and I am climbing up them,
out of the Tube on my way to the park, carrying my drawstring
swimming bag. I know immediately that it is her. It is both a
surprise – a dislocation in time and place, a resurrection of the
ancient past – and not a surprise in the least. On the contrary.
I have been thinking about her for twelve and a half years,
when I wasn't thinking about Nancy. Cynthia too, of course.
But mostly Nancy. This encounter seems as much overdue as
anomalous. It is as if my resentment has beamed her across
Europe, conjured her to life, back into my life, here in the
shade of the museum's plane trees. She does not see me.

I take a few dumbstruck steps before I am shaken into
action by the offer of a leaflet on Creationism. I stop, turn and
follow her, doubling back down the stairs and bounding into
the underpass. Straight away I am surrounded by a swarm of

day-tripping children, seven or eight years old, dressed in high-visibility jackets and accompanied by jittery minders. I am fearfully conspicuous, my body oafish and exposed amid their waist-high forms. I worry that she will see me or, conversely, that I will lose her. There is an exit at the left of the passageway – she could be up and out in a moment. The pursuit feels like a nightmare of impotence, the kind in which one knows one must run for one's life but is unable to move or resist, helpless and waiting for the end.

Members of the Diplomatic Service must not, without relevant authorisation, disclose official information which has been communicateded in confidence within Government.

I can still picture her dancing on Independence Square. I can see her in the underground bar we visited, through the arch on Khreshchatyk, laughing. In the embassy, pleading. She was frightened, of course, one could see that, though perhaps not as frightened as she ought to have been.

She doesn't take the exit. Of course she doesn't. She does not know that I am behind her. Quite possibly she has not thought about me in a decade.

It's all a matter of smell. That's what the office told me. As if that craven rationale were a consolation for what happened.

I sidestep the children and a busker in a cravat. I hurry beneath the strip lights that run along the ceiling, giving the tunnel the air of a hospital or an asylum. I lose her as the passage curves into the station but, dodging the scruffy tourists eating their sandwiches in the ticket hall, I spot her again. Black boots, blue jeans, canvas shoulder bag, a tightish black shirt, understated but not inelegant. Without question, it is her: the aquiline nose, that ebony hair, her eyes. Her eyes, above all.

She passes through the ticket gates and steps onto an esca-lator. I descend behind her, several men in suits and a run of ghastly electronic adverts for a department store between us. Twelve and a half years, and she is indubitably an attractive woman, with that self-possessed bearing that distinguished her even then. I ignore a 'No Entry' sign, almost colliding with a pair of teenagers in replica football shirts coming the other way, and cut through onto the platform.

I am in luck: she has just missed a train. Four minutes till the next one, the departure board informs me. I can hear my footsteps echoing along the tunnel. Perhaps she can hear them, too. But she does not turn.

Ours was not a very long acquaintance, in the scheme of things. Three weeks? Two, maybe. Yet certain episodes swell in one's memory, do they not? Romances, holidays, university exams, incandescent friendships, or, in this case, a connec-tion for which no ready label exists, even if – with her connivance – others were quick to affix one.

Please. You know he will never leave the square. You know it. Please.

Four minutes.

I have often asked myself if what I did in Kiev was wrong. Some of the allegations were lies, of course, pure calumny, but parts of the story were accurate in principle if not in detail. Quite possibly, I erred. I don't only mean 'wrong' in the sense that I violated the code, nor even because of what my actions cost me. I mean that in hindsight it might have been better, for everyone, if she and I had never been involved that night – better than the bloodbath that came later, the war the Krem-lin hallucinated into reality, the rubble. No good deed goes unpunished, as the saying goes, but there is a prior problem, in my view, namely how – in a world, a life, so knotted and capricious, in which the consequences of one's actions can so utterly contradict the intent – how, in such a world, can we ever know what the good deed is?

I recall what Kovrin told me when we negotiated in his car. Losing would only make his side angry, he said that day. Already he had done much more of everything than most people ever do of anything, and certainly more than I ever will. He had been poorer and richer, he had fought more and – doubtless – fucked more. Killed more, possibly. He was right about his associates, one has to acknowledge that. He knew them better than we did.

For this type of person, is not competition. For this type of person, this is war.

All those slogans about Europe and freedom seem rather quaint now. Soon enough, the old faces came back. No dreams came true.

We will not be defeated!

I should never have gone to that bar with her.

The children from the underpass are chuntering onto the platform. One of their minders is trying to keep them back against the wall, waving a clipboard, valiant chap, but they keep vibrating towards the tracks, daring each other, showing off. She is twenty paces ahead of me, on the other side of the electronic board. She always looked cold, out on the streets and in the snow. Her coat was too thin.

A cleaner in a fluorescent yellow jacket is ambling along the platform at penitential speed, and I follow in his wake. A man in heavy boots, paint splattered on his knuckles, is asleep on one of the perforated metal seats. Everyone else seems preoccupied by their phones. I register the CCTV camera that captures the spot where she is standing. I have an urge to wave at it.

Two minutes, now, until our train.

Fate is strange, isn't it? Had I not come out of the tunnel at that exit, I would not have had this chance. I like to walk to the park that way, among the museums, with their aura of accomplishments beyond revision and dispute, past the tourist maps that say *You are here*, as if that were a question which could be settled so glibly. The effect is bittersweet, of course, but I like to pass by the embassies. I imagine that inside, somewhere, they know me – and, in a manner of speaking, forgive me.

I am not at all sure what this is a chance of. Nothing is to be gained, though equally, after Kiev, there is little left for me to lose.

She was on good form, the last time I saw her. Nancy, I mean. Naturally I didn't realise that it might be the last time. It is a species of grief, I think, the feeling I have for my daughter. If I am right, and if what I feel for her is grief, then my experience suggests that reincarnation is real, only it happens among those left behind, not to the people they have lost – the survivors being transformed and left to grapple with their new selves, like the proverbial blind man feeling out an animal in the dark.

... must not disclose official information which has been communicated in confidence ...

One minute, says the board. On the wall across the tracks are adverts for holiday idylls that I will never see. I am five metres away, then three.

Encountering this woman in such a gilded corner of London, a narrative of her life suggests itself to me – a ride on another kind of escalator, from the revolution to politics to the sponsors of politics. Perhaps betraying me was her entrée to a milieu of string-pulling money men and ill-gotten luxury. I imagine her stepping down from one of those stucco-fronted Knightsbridge palaces with their iron railings, the pompous portico flanked by bay trees, or emerging from a turreted red-brick mansion block near the Royal Albert Hall. I wonder why she didn't take a taxi.

In any event, here she is, standing behind the yellow line at the edge of the platform, looking at the floor. And here I am, too. We are all mere atoms – are we not? – pinballing around this world, now and then colliding, providentially or violently, as we two have again today, underneath London.

The idea arrives late, I have to say, but with a kind of gravitational pull. I expect it happens all the time. Crowded platform, a cry, then the lugubrious announcement, the wearily inconvenienced commuters. Probably people get away with it all the time. The CCTV camera might be obstructed by the 'Way Out' sign. Who, in any case, would they be looking for? A non-descript man in late middle age, with a somewhat overgrown beard, in grey trousers and a postman shirt, plus a bag he had been carrying up to the Serpentine for the jolting swim that reminds him, as pain best does, that he is still alive.

I anticipate someone, a minute from now, pressing the emergency buzzer on the wall amid the screams. One of the child-minders possibly. I cannot see the woman's face but I am close enough to smell her: a citrusy tang, rather antiseptic for a perfume, with an undertow of sweat, as if she has recently been in bed with someone.

Her eyes reminded me of Nancy's eyes.

No minutes – the numerical column on the board goes blank. The time left to us is too meagre to measure. My life depends on this moment, yet I also know that this moment has become my whole life. I am tipsy with adrenalin yet serene, as when, at the top of a mountain, one senses that nothing could be more beautiful, more fitting a consummation, than to leap into the sky.

A doomed rat zigzags around the tracks.

*** STAND BACK, admonishes the board. TRAIN APPROACHING ***

I feel the spooky tunnel breeze and hear the rattling crescendo of the train. I see the glow of its headlights on the tunnel wall.

2. The annexe

24 November

AT THE end of her shift in the Lenin Museum she went to look for Andriy. She found him in the basement, heaving crates of bottled water into a storeroom.

'I already told you, no.'

'But I said you would come.'

On a mattress at Olesya's feet, a drowsy woman flailed an arm across her face.

'Someone like him – do you really think he will listen to us?'

'Andriushka, please.'

Protesters were still arriving from Odessa and Lviv and Ternopil – young, most of them, knowing no one in the capital, thousands every day. In the improvised HQ in the museum they were fed from a vat of *vareniki*, saw a doctor if they needed one, and slept in the corridors if they were tired. Andriy volunteered in the goods depot and for the security team, Olesya in the room of blankets. She made tea in an enormous silver urn.

'Are you scared?' Andriy asked his sister. He spat out the name: 'Of Kovrin.'

'It's only talking, what can he do to us? And the British will be there.'

'If you're scared, I'll go with you.' The woman on the floor rolled over. 'Otherwise, there's been enough talking. In my opinion.'

'I'm not scared, I just prefer to have you with me. Always together, remember?'

'I remember,' he said. 'But I won't come. I can't.'

Andriy turned to pick up a crate, but as she reached the stairs he called out to her. 'Be careful, okay?'

'You too,' she said. 'Don't tell Mama.'

Olesya hesitated at the top of the museum steps, an orange steward's band on the left arm of her coat. She breathed deeply in the cold air. The sky was dirtying towards dusk.

We will not be defeated!

She negotiated the icy steps and walked to the agreed spot, near the Philharmonic building on the corner of Volodymyr-sky Descent. Thibaut was standing beside an SUV – black with windows tinted to match – wearing a tailored coat and an aviator-style hat.

'Miss Zarchenko? You got my text. Excellent,' he said in his air-miles accent – Bern via Brussels, with a hint of German internships and a trace of American business school. Thibaut was a citizen of his offshore bank account. He gave a curt, heel-clicking bow.

A steel band had occupied the grass verge between the Philharmonic and the Dnipro hotel in solidarity with the pro-test. The drummers struck up – an iambic one-two, like the beating of a heart – but quickly the rhythm was submerged in chanting from the square.

Shame! Shame!

'Mr Davey is here already. Shall we?'

Glory!

Thibaut opened the car's rear door. Olesya paused, as if she were mounting a tumbril. She removed her armband and got in.

'Good evening,' Simon said, pinching his knees together to ensure their legs didn't touch.

'I thought ... Miss Drayton is not coming?'

'Just me tonight, I'm afraid.'

On the phone, Thibaut had made it clear that Jacqui was too junior to be invited. Naturally the ambassador herself was welcome, but she had deemed it politic to let Simon, her deputy, go alone. The optics; the appearance of neutrality. 'Right,' Jacqui had said when Simon told her. 'If you say so.'

'It's clear,' Olesya said to Simon in the car. 'I have only you.'

Thibaut rapped the dashboard with his gloves. 'Let's go.'

The driver skirted the football stadium and made for the river, the cupolas of the Pechersk sanctuary glinting in the treeline, the mummified holy men reposing nearby in their catacombs beneath the hoard of Scythian gold. They wound down the hill to the embankment. A flotilla of vehicles flying orange banners advanced the other way across the bridge; on a downstream bluff loomed the floodlit statue of the Motherland, blankly wielding her sword and shield. On the other side of the gunmetal water they entered a canyon of Soviet high-rises, diminutive churches huddling between the towers, and beyond that the low-slung normalcy of mobile-phone kiosks, delivery men, streets filled with people who had no wish to be warriors of history, nor to be its casualties.

The driver picked up speed. Snow had settled on the firs that lined the road out of the city, the bark glowing in the headlights, and on the bone-white birches. The limbs of the trees were blotchy with birds' nests. Traffic policemen stood at the roadside, toting the batons they used to flag down their marks. They knew better than to trouble a vehicle like Kovrin's.

The car passed the final street lamp. Olesya clasped the handle above her window.

'If I may,' Simon asked, 'how long have you worked for Mr Kovrin?'

'Two years as executive assistant.' Thibaut swivelled to face him. 'But I started in the investment team.'

'Evidently you distinguished yourself. And where were you before?'

'The MBA, then a venture capital firm in Chicago. They sent me to Baku – hotel developments, mostly.' Thibaut had advert-ready teeth and lineless skin.

They left the highway. The headlights illuminated a cluster of derelict farm buildings and, closer to the road, the carcass of a tractor. A dog bolted in front of the car, heading for a cor-rugated barn. They came to a white fence, built to resemble the perimeter of a Texan ranch, with another fence glowering behind it, electrified mesh with barbed-wire crenellations. Security cameras were mounted at hundred-yard intervals. Olesya craned her neck to watch a camera track them as they passed. She swallowed, then stared ahead, at the driver's buzz cut, Thibaut's arm resting on the leather console between the front seats, and the darkness that was engulfing the road.

'Yesterday,' Simon said, 'on the square, Mr Kovrin implied that he had something in particular to say. I wonder, do you have a sense of the agenda?'

'I'm sure he will explain.' Thibaut grinned. 'Here we are.'

The driver extracted a walkie-talkie from the glove compartment and mumbled a password. The gates of the estate swung open, glacially. They edged through and the entrance closed behind them, resealing the kingdom of money. Simon met the driver's eye in the rear-view mirror. He smiled ingratiatingly but the man did not respond. The embassy knew where he had gone. He straightened his tie.

The driveway led to an English-style manor house, with a gravelled courtyard and a fountain that had been disconnected for the winter. The front door remained closed between its columns; instead, as they stepped onto the gravel, sharp air biting their cheeks after the cocooned warmth of the car, a figure emerged from a different door, in a one-storey annexe at the end of the facade, a hand raised and waving above his head. Another figure, a woman, stood in the annexe's doorway, silhouetted against the light behind her.

'My friends,' Kovrin exclaimed. He crunched towards them, wearing a tight-fitting black polo neck like a commando's. 'Come inside from cold.'

Kovrin ushered them into the annexe, which, like a country cottage, was bedecked with hunting trophies and Afghan rugs. He appraised Olesya as she undid her coat, up from scuffed boots to jeans to turtleneck and back again, just once, very fast, his tongue running wolfishly around his teeth. Olesya noticed and turned away. She withdrew her hands inside her woollen sleeves.

'So,' Kovrin said. 'Please.'

He shooed his guests to a table in front of the fireplace, urgently, as if his home were a restaurant that would need the space back soon. Thibaut set his chair a few subordinate inches back from the others.

'From my point of view, this is nicer,' Kovrin said. 'Nicer than our big house.'

'You have a lovely home,' Simon said.

Olesya scanned the doors and windows. 'I never saw such a house.'

They stood up almost immediately when Natalia Kovrina came in. She was dressed in velour slacks and a pink hoodie, but was coiffed and made-up as if she were preparing for a party. Straight away she embraced Olesya, whose eyes met Simon's across Natalia's shoulder. A pointillist watercolour hung on the wall between a stag's head and the internal door.

'We are so proud of you,' Natalia said. 'Our young people.'

'Thank you,' Olesya said warily. 'You're very kind.'

Natalia unclasped her body but held on to her hands. She gazed at Olesya briefly like the mother of a bride, then retired to the main house.

'You see,' Kovrin said, 'you have more friends than you think. I tell my wife how young protester is coming, and she says she must to meet you. She enjoys the fairy tale – the young people, the singing. But to continue from yesterday, Miss Olesya. Tell me more.'

'Tell what?'

'About you.'

Simon encouraged her with a smile and, in Russian, she told them in a rush: about the town she grew up in, the family apartment that had been smaller than Kovrin's annexe, the bribe they had to pay to get her into university. About her father's training as a physicist and work at a dairy farm, her mother's job as a tour guide for ancestor-hunting Americans. How she had managed to find work in a hotel, but had left it to come to Kiev for 'the revolution'; how most of her peers had gone illegally to Italy or Germany to chase a living as nannies or builders, some of them leaving young children behind. She faltered only when recalling how her brother had gone off to the army and had barely spoken for a year when he got out. 'My baby brother,' she said. 'Not such a baby now.'

Thibaut sighed at appropriate intervals. Simon stroked his beard. Kovrin listened, watching her, jiggling a knee and running a thumb over the knuckles of his other hand. He smiled at 'the revolution'.

'It is a typical story,' Olesya concluded in English. 'On the square, everyone knows these stories, everyone has one, they are tired, they want to live as normal people, as I said yesterday. Jobs. No bribes. Like people in Europe.'

'From my point of view,' Kovrin said, 'Europe is very far away.'

'Europe is not only the place. It is an idea.'

'Everywhere is its own place. Fixed on maps, fixed by history.'

'It can be a different place. We can.'

'It can be worse.'

'Worse for you.'

Simon flinched. Kovrin took a sharp, theatrical breath.

'Brave girl.' He smiled again, but fleetingly, like a twitch. 'Miss Olesya, I know what you think about me. Bandit, yes? You think I have everything from corruption. I must tell you, this is bullshit.'

'Mr Kovrin,' Simon interjected, 'with respect, I don't think Miss Zarchenko implied any such thing.'

'You know where I start my business? In markets. Not Dow Jones market – street markets. Train stations. Selling cigarettes, perfumes. On trains, sometimes. Small radios. You, your government' – he turned to Simon – 'you say markets must be free? This was free markets, believe me. Absolutely free.'

'One can quite imagine,' Simon said. 'Survival of the fittest.'

'We are not angels, okay? Not absolutely clean. I am not Hollywood hero, this is a fact. But I paid fair price for everything. Off records? Sometimes more than fair price. It was bankrupt, the coal mine.'

'Almost bankrupt,' Thibaut said.

'I was not born to be loved by all people,' Kovrin continued. 'Camel can go through needle before rich men is loved. But – this is bullshit! You know what they say about my father? They say he was collaborator for Nazis. My father was born in nineteen thirty-two!' Briefly, he cupped a palm over his eyes. He lowered his voice. 'I am sorry, I will defend my honour.'

'It is your right,' Olesya said. 'And we will defend our democracy.'

'Everybody is defending "democracy" now,' Kovrin said, miming inverted commas in the air.

A man in a chef's hat came in from the main house. 'Something to eat?' Kovrin asked them. 'Please, it's no problem. Maybe some cutlets?'

The chef affirmed that cutlets were feasible. The guests declined; Kovrin waved him away.

'Tell me one more thing,' Kovrin said. 'This man, your leader. You think he is such pure angel? Absolutely white, yes? No money coming into this campaign, no promises going out? Shiny armour?'

'I think,' Olesya said, 'that they should not have tried to kill him. I mean, with the poison. The Russians or ... whoever did this to him.'

Simon slid a palm towards her across the table, wagging a discreet warning with his finger. Kovrin raised a finger to his lips. He cleared his throat.

'Come,' he said, 'we walk, yes? Mr Davey. Fresh airs.' He stood up; another man, not the chef, appeared with his coat. 'Thibaut, you stay, keep our lady company. Okay, Miss Olesya? Stay warm. Something to eat?'

'As you say,' Olesya said. 'It's clear.'

She had been the bait, or the aperitif. She slouched in her chair, her hands in her lap, looking very young. Thibaut nudged his chair towards the table.

At the annexe's back door, Kovrin pulled a BlackBerry from his pocket and tossed it onto a side table, gesturing with his eyes for Simon to follow suit. Outside was a gravelled paddock, floodlit like a parade ground. Three guards were waiting for them, wearing ski hats and puffer jackets; one was smoking but dropped his cigarette when Kovrin appeared, grinding it into the gravel with a pointy boot and bending to retrieve the butt.

'We walk, okay? Forwards!'

'As you wish,' Simon said. He buttoned his coat and put his hands in his pockets.

Kovrin strode up a path that led into the trees, crossing out of the arc of light that covered the paddock and entering the darkness. Simon followed, the three bodyguards shadowing him, closely enough to throttle him if necessary.

'Outside is better,' Kovrin said. 'In my own house even, to discuss hot topics, it can be risky. You understand, I think. Is better also without phones; nowadays they can listen with them.'

'Quite,' Simon said. 'Wise to take precautions, especially at the moment.'

In the secure parts of the embassy – in the communications room and in the box – mobile phones were strictly forbidden. Visitors and local staff were forbidden, too. Iain Carson, the security officer, a Scot and former spook, was fierce about the protocols.

'As for this assassination,' Kovrin began. 'Off records? This happened, absolutely. But "who" is technical question only. Somebody trying to kill, somebody trying to scare, Russians, someone else ... Poisoning is a fact, very important fact, but "who" is detail, believe me. Technical question.'

Simon stepped on a twig that snapped with a crack. The snow beside the path was crystallising into ice.

'The method does tend to incriminate Moscow,' he said. 'Their laboratories, though I don't expect you to confirm that. If I may, though, Mr Kovrin – these election results. In some districts – '

'Misha, please.'

' – in some districts, as I'm sure you are aware, there were more votes than people. Dead people voted. Thousands of dead souls. With the greatest respect, it was a mistake for your side to declare victory in the circumstances.'

'Not *my side*,' Kovrin insisted. 'But, in any cases, I agree. Worse than crime, this was mistake. Problem is, no one wants to seem the weakest. Election officials, some little town in our countryside, no one wants to be poor guy who gives to government their worst result. So they go up, the numbers. Up and up. Is very old story. Now there is this problem in the square.'

They came to a gazebo in the woods. The bodyguards fanned out to surround it; the smoker lit another cigarette, the match igniting like a distress flare in the night. Kovrin and Simon sat on the heated benches.

'Again off records?' Kovrin continued. 'Falsifications is also a fact. But, Mr Davey – Simon – in this election, all camps have cheated. Result? Result is that no one can know result. Is not possible. True result does not exist. So – I make suggestion.'

He paused. Simon nodded.

'We know each other, yes? We talk – four, five times. Six, at German embassy. We trust each other?'

Simon coughed a minimal assent.

'You want compromise – international community. A peaceful solution. Me also.' He hunched in his shoulders in a pastiche of harmlessness.

'Please,' Simon said. 'Tell me what you have in mind.'

'Okay. We take away three per cent from government side. For falsifications. Also orange side – two per cent. Okay, one and a half. Maybe one and a half. From my point of view, this is fair.'

There was a silent interlude of mental arithmetic. 'In which case,' Simon said, 'the opposition would still lose?'

'Yes, he loses. But he loses beautifully.' Kovrin flourished a hand in the air. 'With no violence, you understand? Tell your ambassador, please, tell the Americans – you know them, I think, their guys.' Again Simon nodded. 'This situation now, it's very dangerous. Bad for everyone. For business.'

He did not specify for whom he was speaking. He did not need to.

'With pleasure. But I'm afraid this won't be considered a very enticing offer – the opposition wants a new election, as you heard on the square. And I should point out that this is not our decision, nor the Americans'.'

'Of course,' Kovrin said. 'Is domestic matter only.' Power – he spoke for power. 'Tell them and we can negotiate. Final thing: do you have children, Mr Davey?'

Simon paused. 'One child, yes.'

'Where is he?'

'She. At school, in England.'

They had met at diplomatic receptions and at galas for Kovrin's orphanage charity and the libraries he sponsored; this was the first time Kovrin had pried. *Do not share personal information*, that was the office's advice. They could use it against you. They will.

'I have children. Two boys. All I have, all my businesses, will be for them. They are young now, but one day. My little boys. Listen now, what I am saying. You know this old ... not joke ... proverb: *My friends are near, but my belly is nearer.* No? So, my businesses are nearer. Nearer than these big dramas.'

'Very expressive,' Simon said. 'I think I understand what you're getting at.'

'From my point of view, when this election story is finished, there must be rules of the game. For business – who gets, who keeps. Whoever will be president, with rules of the game, I personally can accept.' He looked Simon in the eye. 'You understand me?'

'Rules of the game. We will bear that in mind. Useful to know where you stand.'

They walked back towards the house. The white ground shone where the moonlight slanted through the trees. 'You know why I prefer this little house?' Kovrin asked, veering towards the annexe. 'Reminds me from my childhood. My father. Not absolutely similar, of course. There we shared our bathroom, kitchen. You've seen these places? Each family, one toilet seat. This little one, inside – I like her, brave girl, she has spirits – she thinks she knows, but she doesn't know. My father, my mother – for my mother I was too late ...' He clasped his jaw, running his gloved fingers across his stubble. 'So, I like it.'

Inside, Kovrin kissed Olesya's hand, bowing so that the visitors made out his incipiently balding crown. 'Absolutely pleasure.' To Simon he said, 'My regards to your ambassador.' He took some papers from Thibaut and vanished into the main house.

The driver was waiting for them at the front of the annexe, a half-moon scar visible on his temple in the light from inside. 'I may join you?' Thibaut said, not really asking.

When they were through the gates and back on the road, the driver turned on the radio, buzzing the dial until he hit the lone independent station. They were interviewing Tina Vlasych, an ally of the poisoned candidate, who, after spending most of her life in upstate New York, had repatriated to her parents' homeland for the orange campaign. It was her job to assure Westerners that if the tarnished election results were set aside, corruption would cease, smuggling would be extirpated, all their aid money would be disbursed wisely.

'The people,' Vlasych was saying, 'will defend their choice to the end. The people will not be silenced!'

'The people!' spat the driver. He turned the radio off.

Simon looked across at Olesya. 'Well done,' he said.

'Will it help?' She looked tired. The rings around her eyes seemed to be deepening.

'How does your saying go? *We wait and hope.* It's important to show them that you are reasonable people.' His arm moved to reassure her, but he withdrew it before he touched her. 'We tried this sort of thing when I was in Tel Aviv – invited some folk from the West Bank to the embassy, got them talking to the Israelis. Neutral subjects, you know – science, education. It's harder to hate someone you've met. Or fear them.'

They drove back to the city. Near where the columns of street lamps began they saw six truckloads of soldiers sheltering under a bridge, three on either side of the road, men in padded vests visible through the open rear flaps. A commander stood on the tarmac, his back to the traffic, speaking on his phone. Inside the trucks, metallic hardware glinted between the benches.

'What's that?' Olesya said. 'What do they have there?'

'Water cannon, I think,' Simon said. 'Probably water cannon. They say it's a training exercise.'

'But it's not,' Olesya said. 'Is it? It's not.'

Thibaut shifted awkwardly in the front seat. Olesya swallowed. She rubbed the bicep on which she wore the orange armband for her volunteer shifts, as if it were bruised.

They thanked the driver when he drew up outside the Philharmonic. He grunted and pulled wordlessly away. Thibaut put on his leather gloves and aviator hat, clicked his heels in farewell and set off in the direction of parliament.

The crowd had swollen almost as far as the junction, dancing together, praying together, ready to march together when they were asked to. A roar went up as the dissident chocolate tycoon came to the stage. 'Dear friends ...'

We will not be defeated!

As if saying it often enough would make it true.

A figure waiting at the bottom of the museum steps, arms clasped around his torso, began to advance towards them.

'Well,' Olesya said, smiling as she recognised Andriy. 'We lived through it.' She shook Simon's hand and pulled on her mittens. 'My hello to Miss Drayton.'

Simon watched as Olesya crossed the road to intercept her brother. She rested her head on his chest.

ii. The envelope

IN THE end, one doesn't jump off the mountain, does one? However liberating the plunge might seem. One peers over the precipice, envisaging the fall, only to straighten up, shudder, and return to the trail and the gratingly oblivious company. The jump never happens, it is not a real event, but one knows, secretly, how close it was. How precarious all of this is. One knows. I know.

The doors open, the vertiginous moment is past, and we weave onto the train. Hours to go, still, before rush hour, but the carriage is cluttered with people on their way to the airport: businessmen with their standard-issue wheelie bags, parents already deploying the heavy-reserve iPad against their square-eyed children, a pair of enamoured students, her head on his shoulder, sleeping. These mysterious other lives.

She sidesteps between them and stands in front of the double doors, one hand gripping the rail above her head, the other clutching her shoulder bag. I lean against the Perspex panel at the end of the carriage. Naturally I am ashamed,

I am penitent over the non-event, but also, I confess, I feel a kind of awe, almost – *mirabile dictu!* – an inkling of self-respect. Mine has largely been a predetermined life, I now see, beginning with a frictionless run from school to university to one of half a dozen plausible professions, and yet I always considered myself a man of action. A good man in a crisis – that is how I was regarded. Drop me in the soup, in over my head, and I would stand firm. One little shove on the platform just now, and a warped version of that dynamic man, that me, would have been resurrected.

In truth, we never really know how close we come to jumping, do we? An inch this side of the edge may in actuality be a mile. Nor, at any given moment, how close those around us may be.

Preposterous, of course. I never would have hurt her. Of course not.

More passengers board and straphang between us, and I have to peer around and between them to keep sight of her. The train emerges from the tunnel, natural light floods in, a shift that always makes me self-conscious, obscurely embarrassed, like a dimmer switch being turned up at the end of a disco. We pull into a station and I notice the electricity cables slithering along the tracks, at once sinister and fragile. I have a belated urge to conceal myself, a nauseous apprehension that I am not ready, but the bodies between us are disembarking, a gaggle of teenagers through the doors opposite her, a crew of builders through the one nearest me. Eventually they are out and I see that she has turned towards me. Her eyes meet mine.

Between two people something can happen, and even if no one else knows about it, it still happened, it's still real.

Or so we agreed that winter.

I almost smile but manage not to. She looks away, then back, then away again, training her eyes on the ground. I am not certain that she has recognised me. Her features were always somewhat angular and severe, but from this distance they seem to have grown gaunt, almost cadaverous. If she has aged, however, so have I. She is still young, still at the stage when her body is her ally, whereas in the time since we last saw each other, in the embassy – no, on Independence Square – I have advanced from early middle age towards its terminus. When one is a child, it seems to me, one is one's body, the sum of what it can do. Then comes the alliance phase, when one is separate from one's body but operating in concert. Next, amid the paunches and receding hair, the body becomes a sort of roommate or half-trusted colleague, only intermittently cooperative. Then – now – it is an enemy, bent not only on thwarting but destroying me. The backache and cholesterol, the gum disease and cancer scares. Skin. Bowel. I will soon be sixty.

They are coming to the square. Soon they cross the river.

The beard, my salt-and-pepper hair, a stature an inch or two above small: in outline I am still the man she would remember from that night. A fateful night, if not quite in the way that it first seemed, since in the end the fate sealed most conclusively was my own. Sealed, that is, by her.

Perhaps she is too far away to be sure. She does not turn again.

She gets off the train and I follow her, out into the daylight and engine roar, heading for the river. Under the flyover, just before the bridge, she leaves the road for a path beside the silver-brown Thames. A young man sitting on a wall, jacket slung over his shoulder, ogles her as she passes (a habit of so many men, when one comes to notice it). Between the yummy mums, the joggers and the early-doors drinkers, there are plenty of people for me to hide behind, should I need to. But she does not look back.

She leads me through a riverside park and a narrow alleyway. On the far side of the alley, where the path joins the road, she buzzes the gate and mounts the steps of a sumptuous Georgian home. The house has a shoulder-high brick wall on the road, topped by iron railings and climbing roses, with a garage entry shaped into the brickwork, its steel front rolled down. Latticed balconies protrude from the first-floor windows. A Mercedes sports car rides up on the pavement.

This is it, I surmise. This is where she lives her magazine-spread life – her well-connected beau washing his money in this mansion beside the Thames, perhaps skedaddling to the Cayman Islands every other month for tax purposes, while she waxes and shops and rationalises the surrender of her principles. She did not seem the type for such a life, with all her high-flown ideals. Not in the least. But if there is one lesson my defunct career has taught me, it is that nothing human beings do should ever be surprising. People change. The endings of their stories turn out only to be beginnings. Characters recur in altogether different guises. In this case, for example, the heroes of Independence Square degenerated into bandits. The routed bandits rallied. The Russians alone were consistent. That winter, they were only warming up. Honing their meddlesome repertoire.

I walk on another twenty yards and lean against the wall of a private garden on the water, beneath an antique street light.

If I rang the bell, and swore to make no trouble, I doubt I would be admitted. A place like that, there will be a house-keeper. Security on tap. And how would I explain?

On the television news, after the murderer is convicted, the relatives always say, 'It isn't enough, my loved one is gone for ever.' Melodramatic, I know, but that is how I feel about her. *This person ruined my life.*

The door opens again and I scuttle around the lamp post. I stroke my beard. My tradecraft would not, I suspect, impress our head of security at the embassy. Briefly the hallway is visible – a mirror, a dark figurine that might be a Modigliani, a housekeeper in a pinafore and a square-suited man, both facing away from me – and then, unexpectedly, she re-emerges, tucking an envelope into her shoulder bag as she descends the steps.

Perhaps this is not her house after all. She does not look round as she retreats through the alley and the park, past the piers and the houseboats, the sun out on the water, a dog sitting alone on a boat ramp across the river. Ahead of us, caught in traffic, a bus stands on the bridge as if it were posing for a postcard. A crane bosses the sky beyond. Back we go, into the dirty real world, back into the station and onto the platform.

A train arrives and we get on again, half a carriage apart. The swimming bag in my hand seems to belong to another era. We head further west, vestiges of countryside breaking out along the embankments, shrubs and wildflowers, like a trapped army escaping a siege.

I will get off at the next stop. I will go home to the flat and out to work in the car this evening. There is an odd consolation in the silent company of strangers, who do not know me and never will. I keep my distance from Whitehall, where there is a chance, however microscopic, that I will be recognised by a fare.

I would never have harmed her, surely not. A peep over the cliff edge only.

Or, I will march along the carriage and corner her against the doors. You will shortly discover, I shall tell her, that in middle age your life becomes a species of country-house mystery. The cast is all the people you know – friends, siblings, rivals – and the object is to determine who will be next to succumb, to illness or booze or divorce. Twelve years ago, I shall say, thanks to you and your lies, the next wreck was me. Us.

Mum's already told me, Nancy said.

I know, popsicle, but I want you to hear—

She told me everything.

There's another side to the story, just, if you'll let me—

But I already know your side of the story, don't I. Remember?

I wanted to convey to Nancy that, in Kiev, my experience of the woman on this train was like a dream you might have about a person you are missing – in this case, Nancy herself – which you are aware is a dream, but are glad of all the same. People can play that role in our lives, can't they? Substitution, projection, call it what you will. I missed my daughter then, but now she is not merely absent but lost, and, as mourners must, I am learning that loss is not one thing but many, since what is gone is not a snapshot of a person but every version of them, past and future, including those she has yet to become. Nancy on the day she was born, birthmarked and furious, the adult she is now, the mother she might one day be. Might already be, for all I know.

When she was at boarding school, I recall, I had a picture in my mind of her going up to university, indulgently dining with me after I drove up to see her in a play – at school she was Malvolio, we managed to get back for it, she brought the house down. In those days Nancy wanted to be something in the theatre, a producer or a set designer, she said she knew she wasn't starry enough to act. Naturally I demurred.

Remember.

I do not get off. I do not shout. The train passes between serried rows of gardens dominated by washing lines, trampolines and outsized sheds. Above the roof line, a plane that had been coming in to land disappears into a cloud. A stray rucksack is propped, unchaperoned, beneath the interconnecting door. I see her scanning it warily, as these days people do. She tucks loose hair behind her ear.

I move between the seats, heart shaking with blood, not breathing, gliding somehow, and stand by the doors. I stare at her, in such a way that the subject of the stare must always register before long, according to some primitive mammalian instinct.

There is a full-blown opera in her eyes. They widen in their bruised rings, close, avert themselves, dart around in an attempt to get away, like a desperado trying all the exits in a blazing house. Eventually the eyes come back to me. She is shocked by this ambush, it seems, disoriented by the ghoulish apparition from her past, but I do not think that she is scared. Not really, or not yet. She swallows.

'I thought, it couldn't be you,' she says. Her voice is unchanged, throaty like the growl of a smoker, though I never knew her to be one. She is bone pale. 'It's been so many years, I wasn't certain.'

'Yes,' I say, 'it's me.' The effort to control my voice flattens it into strangeness. 'Do you remember?'

'Of course, I remember.' She breathes sharply through her nostrils, fists clenched. 'What do you want?'

'I want to talk, that's all. Just talk.'

Her hands relax. She closes her eyes and nods. 'Okay, Simon. We will talk.'

3. Yellow roses

26 November

A CASSOCKED priest held aloft an Orthodox cross. An old man bore a gilt-framed icon, exposing the sombre painted saint to the damp air. After them trailed a posse of government supporters, emitting a vodka haze as they slalomed between the tents and the chestnut trees on Khreshchatyk. The opposition throng tactfully made way for them.

'It's Andriy, isn't it? Can you talk for a minute?'

A team of orange stewards were escorting the counter-protesters to make sure there were no scuffles. Jacqui recognised Andriy among the minders.

She had asked in Russian but he answered in English. 'Who is this?'

'Jacqui Drayton, do you remember? From the British embassy, I met you at the university.'

He broke off from the cordon. 'It was summertime? Yes, I can remember.'

Andriy wore an orange band on the arm of his leather coat, jeans tucked into combat boots left over from his army service, a black hat pulled over his ears. He was twenty-one but his eyes looked older.

'My colleagues,' Jacqui said. 'Simon Davey, Iain Carson.' She indicated the men with a desultory flutter of her wrist.

'How do you do?' Simon said.

'Pleasure,' Iain said, looking harmless in his bulky coat, like a grandparent on the touchline. They did not shake hands.

'They're behaving?' Simon asked. 'These government people. Might be looking for trouble, parading through your territory like this.'

'So far, no problems,' Andriy said. 'They pay them, they come, take photos for newspaper, go home. No provocations. For that, they don't pay enough.'

His Adam's apple bobbed above his leather collar as he tracked the icon and the cross. They vanished among the tents.

'Pleased to hear it,' Iain said. Earlier he had come down alone to gauge the mood.

'We do nothing neither. Everyone is cold. Time we should go.'

'Go where?' Jacqui asked him.

'Go, take parliament, take government house. Take it when all our people are still here. Until now this is like some party – dancing, singing. We wait too long.'

'On the contrary,' Simon said, 'the longer you keep this up, the more pressure they are under. The Supreme Court is hearing your challenge to the election results; it may only be a few days—'

'We should take parliament.' Andriy's nose was running from the cold but he didn't wipe it. 'Take court.'

The aroma of borscht wafted from the street kitchens. 'Right,' Jacqui said. 'Well.'

'Olesya,' Simon said, 'your sister, is she here this evening?'

'They are making little march today,' Andriy said. 'Up to presidential administration, eight o'clock. For cameras only.' His tone softened. 'Keep eyes on her, okay? I must stay here, on Khreshchatyk – now is my time on our rota. So watch her, okay? Please.'

'Of course,' Simon said. 'Don't worry.'

'Good lad,' Iain said. But Andriy was already walking away.

They waited on the corner of Instytutska Street while the marchers assembled. At the front, alone, was the firebrand politician with the braid, a woman who had never met a rabble she had not tried to rouse. Behind her, an army of supporters was mustering on the edge of the square and along Khreshchatyk.

'Got to keep the blood flowing,' Iain said. 'Can't have your foot-soldiers getting bored. You know, there's a textbook on this peaceful-revolution business – they wrote it in Serbia, these probably downloaded it from the internet.'

'Yes,' Jacqui said. 'I know that.'

'Russians are terrified that someone'll try it there. That's why they want this lot squashed. Make an example of them.'

A dozen young women were stationed between the politician and the crowd, each bearing a yellow rose, lined up like sacrifices to a gluttonous Greek god. Some held their roses across their chests like breastplates; others, wilting under the attention, dangled the flowers by their sides.

'Clever chaps,' Iain said. 'They'll have to knock down the lasses to get to the rest.'

'Very chivalrous,' Jacqui said.

'There she is,' Simon said softly. 'There's our friend.'

Olesya stood near the end of the row. She was talking to the woman beside her, and smiling, but as she turned away, towards the footbridge and the cobbled road that ran uphill from the square, her expression suggested helpless bafflement, as if she were waking up in an unfamiliar bed, retracing her steps, deciphering how she had wound up here, on the front line, armed with a rose.

Simon waved, a discreet, waist-level rotation of his leather-gloved hand that she did not appear to see. Only Jacqui saw. He opened his mouth as if to call out but did not find the words.

'Rather a risk, don't you think?' he said instead to Iain. 'Administration's pretty jittery up there, by all accounts.'

'It's hardly a raiding party,' Iain told him. 'They're marching up the hill and down again – grand old Duke of York. But then they win either way, don't they?' Iain gurgled the phlegm in his throat. 'Beauty of it. The lasses get bashed up, they've won. Brutal dictatorship, you know, outcry all over the world. Don't get bashed up, the mob up the hill'll look weak. So.'

The command to advance came down from the stage. Heroic music throbbed from the loudspeakers but most of the marchers were quiet. The diplomats kept to the pavement, below the concert hall in which the NKVD had shot people during the purges, scurrying alongside the TV crews like raggedy camp followers. The road was steep, and Iain began to pant and mutter to himself: 'On you go … good lad … good lad.' He bent forward as if for a rugby scrum, grimacing so that his grey-blond moustache curled cartoonishly upwards.

They passed the shuttered Metro station. A papery snow began to fall. 'Bugger,' Iain said, doubled over, his hands on his knees.

'Will you manage?' Simon said. 'We can wait.'

'I'll be all right,' Iain said. 'It's just a stitch.'

The politician with the braid and the line of young women halted in front of the Writers' Union on the corner of Bankova Street, in sight of the white portico of the presidential administration. Their route was barred by armoured trucks and a phalanx of riot police, black-suited, visors down, kitted out like Stormtroopers. The men stood in formation, three rows deep, guns strapped to their sides, barking dogs at their flanks.

A priest emerged from the crowd and approached the barricade, incense smoking from his thurible. 'Over there,' Iain said, gesturing towards the columns of the central bank. 'Cover if we need it.'

'Right,' Jacqui said, ducking her head as she crossed the road, as if the shooting had already started. They were diplomats, observers, officially immune, but also mortal, flesh-and-blood, as penetrable as anyone else if the bullets flew.

Thirty thousand people had mustered for the march, the stragglers were only now leaving the square, but as Olesya and the others neared the riot shields, the confrontation shrank. A dozen women bearing roses faced a hundred armed men. Armed and young, as young as the women, they abashedly inched backwards before halting and stiffening in response to an inaudible command.

'Steady,' Iain whispered.

'My God,' Simon said. 'This could be it.' He stroked his beard and covered his mouth with his hand.

'Don't throw anything, comrades,' Iain said. 'Don't fucking fart.'

One of Olesya's neighbours in the line crossed herself. The woman on her other side held her rose in the crook of her arm, like a lance. The music on the square was a distant hum.

Together we are many!

The politician with the braid and the women with the roses linked arms and stepped towards the barricade. Feet shuffled behind the riot shields. 'Steady,' Iain repeated. 'Steady boys.'

'And girls,' Jacqui said.

The crowd edged together in the near-darkness. The priest murmured. Nobody else spoke.

The women reached the men. In synchrony they stretched out their hands, each wielding her rose, inserting them stem-first into the riot shields' perforations. A barrage of cameras flashed; the disoriented troops looked down, or behind them for instruction, or above the women's heads at the snow fuzzing the asphalt sky.

The marchers began to sing the national anthem. The lyrics swept through the crowd until the women at the front joined in – as, halfway through, did several of the men facing them, their jaws working but their lips covered by their visors.

Upon us, my young brothers, fate shall smile again.

Olesya threw her head back as she sang, her neck stretched and exposed, as if for the knife.

We'll lay down souls and bodies for our freedom.

The anthem ended. Some of the people on the march applauded. Delicately, the young women stepped backwards from the barricade. Simon exhaled.

'Good show, ten out of ten,' Iain said. 'Very pretty on CNN tonight. Shall we now? I'll do better downhill.'

'You two go,' Simon said. 'I'll just have a quick word.'

'The girl,' Jacqui said. 'I really wouldn't mind debriefing her. If it's all right with you.'

'It's no trouble,' Simon insisted. 'I'll fill you in later.'

Jacqui rolled her eyes. She watched him weave into the road to intercept Olesya.

She was gabbing with her neighbour in the line, wired with adrenalin, as if she had landed a skydive or escaped from a bear.

'Hello, Miss Zarchenko? You were ... That was really something.'

'Thank you ... Simon? Thank you. Well, this is Yaryna, my friend.'

'Pleased to meet you,' Yaryna said in Russian. She set a pair of purple earmuffs on top of her blond hair.

'Me too. Simon – Simon Davey.'

'Hello, Simon Davey. Did you see us?'

'I did. And quite a lot of other people will see you on television, I expect.'

'You're the diplomat, is that right? The Englishman.'

'At your service,' Simon said, hamming it up. 'That's me.'

'We were at university together,' Olesya explained. 'We shared a room.'

'We shared many things,' Yaryna said. 'Didn't we?'

'Don't,' Olesya said, elbowing her friend but laughing, from relief as much as at the bawdy allusion. Yaryna laughed too, a laugh that sputtered into a cough that choked into a doubled-over wheeze.

'Is she all right?' Simon said. 'Shall I make a call?'

Yaryna gripped her knees; Olesya put a practised hand on her back. 'Where is it? Yaryna, where is it?'

Yaryna gestured towards the outside pocket of her coat. Olesya reached for the inhaler, shook it and held it to her friend's lips. After the first hit, Yaryna grasped the inhaler and straightened up.

'It's normal,' she said. Her eyes were watering; she took another puff. 'Don't worry. So, I'll see you at the museum?'

The women did a clenched-fist handshake and Yaryna strode away. Olesya monitored the earmuffs as they disappeared down the hill.

'Brave young woman,' Simon said in English. 'Both of you are. Tell me, did they train you for that? I'm curious. The business with the roses.'

'We practised one time this afternoon, down behind this stage. Be like Gandhi, they tell us – be strong and nothing happens.'

Some of the marchers were singing, their voices dwindling towards the square. Simon hesitated. 'I must say, if my own daughter ... she is younger than you, but ... your parents must be very proud of you.'

'Thank you.' She hugged herself against the cold. 'They are not here, only my cousin, I stay on his floor. He lives over the river – they call it the Left Bank, but it's not Left Bank like in Paris. And my brother is here – Andriy.' She blew on her hands.

'Yes, we ran into your brother earlier. Doing his duty.'

'Both of us, our grandmother told us many times, "Do the good thing, or do nothing."'

'That's an excellent lesson.' He coughed. 'Well, if there's ever anything ... if we can help you in any way, I mean afterwards, with your work perhaps, please let us know.'

An officer was megaphoning orders to the riot police. They ambled away from the barricade. 'As a matter of interest,' Simon asked, 'did he say anything to you? The young man opposite you. The riot policeman.'

'Only a little. He asks for my phone number.'

'And did you give it to him?'

She laughed.

They walked downhill together until he lost her in the crowd. As he reached the bottom, the cobbles slick from the snowfall, Simon's phone rang.

'Mr Davey?'

'Speaking.'

'This is Thibaut, do you remember? I wonder – Mr Kovrin wonders – might you be able to spare a few minutes? Only a few minutes.'

Simon cupped his hand around his BlackBerry lest the radioactive name be overheard. 'When would he have in mind?'

'Mr Kovrin wants – he asks – now? If you can be so kind.'

Dorian Thompson wasn't in the foyer of the Hotel Ukraina, so Jacqui tried the restaurant. That was where the journalists tended to congregate, beneath the glittery Soviet chandeliers, when they weren't sidling up to protesters to ask if they spoke English. The TV crews had set up their equipment at the windows behind the buffet. The square pulsed below them like a floodlit coliseum.

Thompson's wasn't among the starry faces in the restaurant. The BBC's chief correspondent was there, and the queenly globetrotter from CNN – the more prominent a news story grew, the higher the stakes and more imminent the carnage, the more inexpert the commentary became. Already the local journalists had been big-footed by brand names like Thompson, dispatched by panicky editors in London and New York. Before long they would ship out the anchors to present the news in earmuffs. Naturally, everyone wanted to interview the ambassador; these days Jacqui doubled as her diary secretary.

She headed for the bar, her boots greasing a trail of slush on the stairs. An old woman with a mop and bucket was vainly cleaning the foyer's marble tiles. Jacqui tried to smile an apology but the woman didn't look up. Groups of protesters huddled on the sofas.

Dorian Thompson was in the bar. He was sitting at a corner table with an expat banker who occasionally rolled up at embassy parties. They did not see her approaching.

'Everyone thinks it's the women, don't they? I mean, that it's the women that keeps us here,' the banker said above the music. 'I'll let you into a secret, Dorian.' He tapped a finger to his veiny nose. 'It's not the women. It's the food.'

'Mr Thompson?'

Shame! rumbled the square below them.

Thompson straightened his grin and stood up. 'Miss Drayton?'

The banker scrutinised her face, as people do when deciphering how embarrassingly they have been overheard. He pretended to check his watch and made his excuses; Jacqui took his seat.

'What can I do for you?' She polished her glasses with her scarf. The cigarette smoke was nauseating.

'Something to drink?' Thompson was wearing a purple fleece, combat trousers and pristine Timberlands. 'Well, thank you so much for coming. What I'm looking for, really, is a little background. Not a place I'm all that familiar with.'

'Right,' Jacqui said. 'Shoot.' She undid her coat but kept it on.

'First of all,' Thompson said, 'the European business. All these EU flags they're waving. What's that about, would you say?'

She sighed. 'Best to ask them. But I would just point out that it means something different than it might at home. The rule of law, clean elections, things that you and I take for granted. Mostly they're just tired of being ripped off – the police, you know, the bureaucrats. The corruption is off the charts. Mr Thompson?'

She followed his gaze, back over her shoulder and through a gauzy curtain to a pole on which a redheaded stripper in a G-string had suspended herself by her ankles. Thompson's view was obstructed by a pillar, such that he was obliged to crane sideways to see. The woman's upside-down face expressed the purest boredom. Her eyes met Jacqui's; neither of them smiled.

Glory! intoned the square.

'Mr Thompson?'

'Sorry. Yes. Sorry.' The struggle between his brain, his eyes and whichever other parts of him were issuing instructions was pitifully legible. A notebook lay on the table in front of him but he hadn't opened it. 'What I meant to say was, would it, do you think, be totally wrong – just hear me out here – would it, you know, be totally inaccurate, to say they were protesting, you know, *against* the European Union? That would make more sense to our readers.' He sipped his wine. 'The desk would prefer it, definitely. What do you think? Okay?'

She closed her eyes. Jacqui Drayton had a PhD from University College London; she had written her thesis on regional authorities in the Soviet Union during the premiership of Leonid Brezhnev. She had put in for other roles at this embassy, and at the one in Moscow – she had wanted and expected to get a political brief – but after the appointments panel, she was given public affairs. Her husband had stayed in London to keep his accountancy job. Here she was, enduring the kind of condescension that, in aggregate, can seem like a conspiracy to do a person down: her name misremembered, instructions barked at her, credit for her initiatives purloined. Shut out of the meetings that mattered, she was stuck in a hotel bar with a catatonic stripper and Dorian Thompson in his war-zone chic.

'I think it would be.'

'Be what – okay?'

'Be factually inaccurate. On background? It's simple really. The government stole the election, the opposition wants a rerun. What we want – this bit, you can quote – is a peaceful outcome that reflects the democratic wishes of the people.'

'Got it.' Now the notebook was open but Thompson hadn't written anything. He gave a leering smile; Jacqui grimaced in anticipation. 'The thing is, I was hoping – we'd really be very grateful – do you think I could see the ambassador later?'

TWO army officers knelt on the stage in the square and pledged their allegiance to the people. The more senior clutched his cap to his breast with one hand and made a patriotic speech into the microphone he held in the other. 'The army is with the people! Glory to you all!'

The army is with the people!

A battalion of snowmen in orange scarfs stood guard on Khreshchatyk. Voices and laughter emanated from the tents as Simon passed them; from one came the half-muffled but unmistakable gasps of lovemaking. They must have heard the rumours. The football stadium in Donetsk was packed with convicts, all sworn to win their freedom in the blood of protesters on the square. Trainloads of drunken roughnecks were chugging towards the capital to wreak havoc on behalf of the regime. Yet here they were, these young idealists, fucking their way to the future.

Gingerly he ascended the ice-glazed steps of an underpass. Outside the currency exchanges the dollar rate was climbing, the red digits ticking over like the timer on a bomb. The wind drove the gritty snow into his face and the scent of petrol into his nostrils. Beset by an uncanny sensation that someone was following him, Simon whirled around, but no obvious culprit was visible. He found Kovrin's car in a turning, opposite a park.

'Mr Davey,' Thibaut said, smiling. 'Good evening.' He opened the rear door, standing beside it as if at attention.

'Something to drink?' Kovrin asked from the back seat. Simon climbed in and the door closed behind him.

'No, thank you.' He lowered his scarf from his chin and smoothed his beard.

'You enjoy the movie?'

'I don't quite follow.'

'Is Hollywood, yes? Is one TV channel covering this stunt – not mine, the channel of the chocolate king. I saw this little one, that one you bring to me at my home. With her flower.'

'I didn't bring her to you, Mr Kovrin. You invited her, as I recall.'

'Very pretty picture, but absolutely Hollywood. My wife, she likes it. My children, my boys, they are watching. Bedtime story. Fairy tale.'

There was a drink in the cup holder in front of Kovrin's seat but he didn't touch it. The driver – a different man, with a spider tattooed behind his ear – remained in the front but did not turn or speak. Kovrin crossed one leg over the other in his pressed black trousers.

'You wanted to see me again,' Simon said. 'I'm listening. Please.'

'Mr Davey, I understand this is negotiation. Absolutely, I understand. Like business. Not *like* business – is business. So, now we make new offer.'

'Mr Kovrin, much as I enjoy our talks, until the Supreme Court rules on the election, I'm not sure there is much to be gained by—'

'Court? From my point of view, court is dangerous. If government side loses, they can be angry. You understand?'

'In a manner of speaking.'

'You know for who court is most dangerous? For judges. Remember this reporter, who makes his investigations of corruption, then they find his body in a forest but no head?'

'I remember all too well. We made our feelings about that very clear.'

Kovrin tutted. Beyond the car's tinted windows people were queuing for hot chocolate from a little chalet in the park, as if nothing in the world were happening.

'Is warning of history, this case. But – off records? – these crowds, such pictures, it means new context, different possibilities. So, I suggest new concept. Very small suggestion.'

Kovrin held his thumb and forefinger in front of Simon's face, half an inch apart. When he saw that Simon was focusing on his hand, he squeezed the digits together, like a vice.

'We make new election. Is okay?'

53

Simon hesitated. Kovrin – they – appeared to be drastically upping their offer: no longer merely a more presentable result, but a rerun, potentially a different outcome.

'But that is precisely what the court is considering. It's their decision, in our view. It's got to be transparent.'

'Absolutely, new election.' Kovrin paused; Simon waited for the catch. 'New election means new candidates.'

There it was.

'Who would these new candidates be, may I ask?'

'This is not important.' He batted a hand as if swatting a gnat. 'Technical question.'

'Mr Kovrin – '

'Misha.'

'With the best will in the world, I very much doubt that would be acceptable. Including to the international community.'

'International community,' Kovrin drawled. He stroked his stubble. 'Mr Davey – Simon – you understand, is risky, this situation. Off records? Anything can happen here. Listen carefully what I am saying. Anything.'

The driver switched on the engine and Simon startled, but the car did not move. The heating came on; Kovrin grinned.

'Look around. You think this is holiday camp? Young Pioneers? The roof there, you see – no, not here, that one, on top of shops – you know what is there? Snipers. You know what is snipers? It's true. I know. All along Khreshchatyk, on these roofs, on post office building. This is not fairy tale, Mr Davey. When night comes, when TV cameras are turned off, absolutely no happy ending. Not roses like today – only guns. It's clear?'

Simon studied the damp patch spreading across the vehicle's carpet from his fur-lined boots. There were subplots

– the courts and the diplomats – but this was a story of blood-shed, averted or impending. Yaryna's blood, Andriy's blood. All of them. Olesya's blood.

'Perfectly.'

A raucous group of protesters romped past the car. *Together we are many!*

'These young people, you think I don't care? I am not such a monster – Simon, Mr Davey – I am man. I am father, like you — we are same age, I think, almost, me and you. From father's point of view, compromise is better. Better for everyone.'

'We can agree on that. Moderation in all things. And I don't doubt your concern, not at all. But in all conscience, as I may already have mentioned, I think you might rather have over-estimated our—'

'We deal not only with you. You think so, because we talk at some parties? Is diversified operation – means we speak to many sides. Only think about this concept, talk again to your Americans. Now.'

The car door opened, pursuant to a signal issued at a fre-quency above Simon's range. 'Our compliments to your wife,' Kovrin said. As Simon stepped down onto the compacted snow, he added, 'And to your daughter.'

Thibaut was still on the pavement in his aviator hat. 'Have a wonderful evening,' he said, smiling. His modish shoes were too flimsy for the weather. He climbed into the front passenger seat and the car pulled away.

Cynthia was already in bed. Simon had checked in at the embassy to brief the ambassador about Kovrin. He had phoned his American counterpart; then he had walked home.

Outside St. Sophia's cathedral, the kiosks that sold religious knick-knacks were closed. He passed the upright piano that stood on the pavement in front of the neighbourhood bar, and the mural of a living room painted in the archway of his building. In his courtyard a hairdresser's was hidden in a basement like a speakeasy, the legacy of some haphazard privatisation in the nineties. The crows congregating at the dumpster ignored him as he punched in the entry code. Dank and shadowy, the doorway seemed purposely designed for ambushes. Finally came the climb to their triple-locked apartment on the third floor, the curlicued swirl of the ironwork incongruous beside the cracked stone and scabrous paintwork of the stairwell. They had inherited the place from the previous DHM. Cynthia hated it.

He called out but she did not respond. He found her in their bedroom, lying in her clothes in the dark, facing a window with a view across the courtyard and into someone else's life. The light from their neighbours' apartments glinted off the falling snow. A silk scarf with an orchid pattern was fixed tightly around her neck, like a cravat, or a noose.

'How was it today, darling? Progress?'

'He cried off,' Cynthia said. 'Everybody's doing that.'

She was working on a pamphlet (or perhaps a book) about seventeenth-century icons, those extant specimens that were saved when the churches were looted or blown up. A priest at the monastery had been supposed to show her its collection.

'I'm sorry. It's a mess at the moment.'

'Yes, I've gathered.'

He sat on the edge of the bed.

'Did you hear from her today?'

'She had a mock – theatre studies. She asked about Christmas.'

'On good form?'

'She wants you to call her.'

Cynthia rallied for dinners and embassy functions – just about, not always – but she hadn't really been happy since they left America. There she had volunteered at an elementary school in Anacostia; she had her garden. Their neighbours had kept a speedboat and they went waterskiing on the Potomac. Simon had been hopeless but Cynthia was a demon.

'Will do. It was quite a remarkable evening, incidentally. A group of young women stormed the presidential administration. Well, not stormed exactly. For a moment we thought there might be carnage. Somehow they reminded me, one of them … It doesn't matter.'

Cynthia had been less than happy, much less, since Tel Aviv.

'Yes, I saw it on television.'

They were almost out of pleasantries. 'Do you need anything?'

'Nothing.'

'Drink?'

'No, thank you.'

'I'll call,' Simon said.

'Do.'

Like all the embassy families, they assumed their apartment was bugged – the local spooks, the Russians, both – but in their case there was very little for anyone to overhear.

'I'll call then.'

He went through to the kitchen, dialled the number for Nancy's house and heard the tell-tell click of the phone-tap. He asked the curt child who answered to fetch his daughter.

'Popsicle, it's Daddy.' Giggling at the other end, a burst of piano practice (Chopin, possibly), plus the hum of the ancient refrigerator beside him in the kitchen. 'Tell me about the mock ... What did Mr Atkins say?' He laughed. 'Good *ad hominem* stuff ... I know you do, popsicle, but I'm afraid I can't say for ... I hope it'll be finished too, but in any case you could come here ... No, I know it won't be the same without Grandpa, I'm quite aware ... No, I haven't forgotten the driving lessons, we'll go out to that aerodrome, there won't be any other cars, I can teach you there ... She's perfectly well ... We'll call again tom—'

His smile held for thirty seconds, the afterglow of love. He screwed his eyes closed, a hand on his brow as he sat in silence at the table.

When he returned to the bedroom, Cynthia had changed into her nightie and retreated beneath the covers. Simon undressed, roped down the blind and slid into bed. He lay on his side, his back to hers, the width of a person between them.

iii. The gasworks

THE TRAIN slows to a predatory crawl. For a minute its rattle and thud are the only sounds in the carriage.

'Olesya,' I say finally, my face close to hers, her face averted, 'why didn't you keep quiet? About what we did that night.'

I am holding the overhead rail with one hand, my swimming bag in the other. She stares through the window in the carriage door.

'It wasn't how you think.'

'And the business about you and me, that we were ... That we ...'

'I told nothing about that. Never, I swear it.'

We reach a station (hers, as it turns out), but she does not bolt. She is not fleeing. On the contrary. She pauses for a heartbeat in front of the open doors, like a parachutist awaiting her turn at the hatch, before stepping onto the platform. We descend to the ticket hall and pass through the barriers. Standing on the litter-strewn pavement in the sunshine, I resume my interrogation.

'Do you have any idea what it cost me? Has that ever crossed your mind?'

'On the square,' she says, 'I tried to tell you—'

'Tell me what?'

She was a warrior that winter, or so it seemed to me. An Amazon. I remember her outstretched hand holding a rose, her breath irradiated by the flash of cameras. I remember, after the court had ruled, finding her on Independence Square, hoisted on a man's shoulders. She must already have persuaded herself that ruining me served a higher cause.

That is a feature of conspiracies, as one infers from spending time in places where they proliferate: they have only to make sense to the conspirators.

'What I am trying to tell you now – that none of this was how it looks to you.'

An ambulance wails past us. 'I saw you,' I blurt out, mistakenly, as I ought to have realised. 'By the river.'

At this – the full extent of my stalking – her eyes widen. Now she is alarmed.

'What did you see?'

'You went into that house and came out with an envelope.'

'Who did you see? Apart from me.'

'No one else, a housekeeper maybe. Is that where you live now?'

'Not anymore.' She fumbles in her bag for her phone but the screen is dead. She sighs. 'I'm sorry, Simon.'

Olesya picks a gap in the traffic and strides across the road. I dodge a motorcycle deliveryman and follow her. She accelerates towards a Polish delicatessen, the nearest open shop. 'Wait, please,' she says at the door. 'A minute, please.'

I do as she asks. Glancing through the window, I see her pleading with a woman inside. The woman scrutinises me, quickly turning away on Olesya's hushed instruction. She picks up her phone.

This time, I act, colliding with a stack of shopping baskets as I barrel inside. 'No,' I say, my knee throbbing from the impact. 'It's okay, really, we're old friends.' My hands are raised in a *Don't shoot!* pose.

The woman is standing behind the meat counter, mince and giblets arrayed in front of her, a basket of headless fish, dried and yellowing, on top of the glass. She turns to Olesya.

'Please,' I say, 'I only ... Remember what we told each other on the square? The two of us, our secret – it was supposed to last for ever.'

It means it's for ever, whatever will be.

'Yes, I remember.' But she isn't looking at me.

'Will I call the police?' The woman wears an unseasonal puffy gilet and professorial glasses on her nose. Her greying hair is twisted above her head in a schoolgirlish band. 'Is it okay?'

'Just talk,' I repeat. 'Please.'

Olesya closes her eyes. 'All right then, we'll talk, you have the right. I think it's okay,' she says to the woman.

Countries need a history – they invent one if they have to – and people are no different. Now is too late to undo the past, as it is everywhere and always, but it is not too late for me to understand it.

'Thank you,' I say. 'I give you my word.'

The woman puts the phone down on the counter.

Outside I trot alongside Olesya as she turns into a down-at-heel high street. A group of rough-looking men – heads shaved, liquor-infused skin – sit gabbing on a low wall outside a church. We pass two policemen, thumbs tucked into their stab-vests, and I half expect her to cry out, but she does not. She walks with the demeanour of someone who hopes that, if she can only avoid eye contact with the world, the world might leave her alone.

'This way,' she says, turning into a park and striding towards a playground. A mother in a billowy black veil and aviator sunglasses rises from a bench and wheels away her infant. 'Here,' Olesya says, sitting down. Safety in the open air, she evidently calculates. 'I'm listening. Tell me what you want.'

A good man in a crisis – that was my reputation. It dated to our first year in Washington, when I deputised at an EU ambassadors' lunch. They were cooking up a tendentious critique of the Americans – something to do with the Bosnian arms embargo, the Pentagon was accused of breaking it – and despite my lowly status I said no. *Nein. Non.* Later, in Kiev, the government claimed to have solved the murder of that unfortunate reporter. 'Throw him to the Chechens!' the old president had allegedly said on a shady tape, and they found him in the forest, doused in acid, minus his head.

The ambassador was on leave, I was chargé d'affaires, and I put out a statement denouncing the whole bleak farce. Any fool could see the investigation was a sham: witnesses were dying in police custody, the real suspects were AWOL. A serious obstacle to bilateral relations, I called it, and straight away the foreign ministry called me in.

This is not how friends should speak about each other. For us, this is a big disappointment.

We're disappointed too, I told the crew-cut apparatchik. *We like our friends to observe the rule of law.*

London heard about that in the diptel. People said, *sotto voce*, that it might not be a bad idea if I were in charge permanently. Then came the revolution – my chance to soar free of the budgets and admin that are a DHM's stock-in-trade. I had a flexibility that the ambassador did not share. I took meetings she could not risk. I knew my American counterpart slightly from our DC days, which made me a useful conduit. Our protestations of neutrality were somewhat disingenuous, but for once our interests and our values were aligned – clean elections, the integrity of the courts, all those arcane pieties. We would punch above our weight, just as, *mirabile dictu*, we once aspired to.

'You know,' I tell Olesya, 'the strange thing was, at the very beginning, I didn't quite appreciate how much trouble you had got me into.'

I raise a palm to quell her protests: if nothing else, she will hear me out.

'Foolish of me, I realise. But I had conducted rather a lot of these disciplinary chats myself, over the years, after some minor security breach or other – mislaid documents or what have you. We would leave a note on our colleagues' desks and they would come to see Iain or me. Pull your socks up, we told them, walls have ears. You remember Iain, I expect?'

She does. 'The man with the moustache? I remember.'

'They wanted to know why I hadn't notified them,' I continue. 'Standard procedure, you see, to tell the security officer about any ... involvement. I could have been blackmailed because of you, that was how they saw it, which made my security clearance ... which meant I couldn't do my job.'

Again I raise a hand to forestall her objection. She wears no make-up, I notice. On reflection I think perhaps she never did, or at any rate very little. Crow's feet creep from the corners of her eyes. The aubergine discolouration below them has become more pronounced, deeper, as if she had been thumped.

'To begin with, they only suggested that I take some time off – simplest way to get me out of the country, I now see. Then they implied that I was being short-toured, and I thought, well, okay, they'll assign me to the consular section in Paraguay or Fiji – that was how this sort of thing was handled in the old days, a whiff of scandal and they packed you off to the other side of the globe.'

'Short what?'

'Brought back from my posting early – which would have been humiliating, but not the end of the world. Perhaps that would have been the worst of it, if the Americans hadn't been so furious. And the press coverage, the newspapers – you must have seen that.'

'Yes, I saw, but I did not speak to any journalists, only—'

'Instead, there was a hearing.'

'You mean, like a court?'

A child in a Spider-Man costume shrieks down a slide behind us.

'Like a court, but for my job.'

There is, in my experience, a weird but reliable phenomenon whereby the most important events in one's life, the most intimate, tend also to feel the least authentic, such that one must struggle to make them one's own. Like those accounts one reads of near-death hallucinations, in which the patients imagine they are looking down at themselves, as if on a stranger, from the hospital ceiling. Losing one's virginity, the vows Cynthia and I took in the church in Sussex, my disciplinary hearing: always, at these moments, I have the sensation that the crisis is happening not to me but to an individual closely resembling me, a doppelgänger who has learned the script and mouths it as I look on.

Thank you for joining us today.

Don't mention it. As if not joining them had been an option.

Do you know everybody?

One of the three adjudicators – the director for the Middle East and Africa, we had been in the same intake – shuffled his papers. The whole business was English in the extreme, smiles as if we were all still chums, the illusion of fair play.

If I may, what is the source of these allegations? About the embassy. About my relationship with the young woman.

I'm afraid the investigating officer is not at liberty to disclose that.

But it's positively Kafkaesque. How am I supposed—

Duty of care. I'm sure you understand.

'You were fired?' Olesya asks me. 'I heard only that you went back to England.'

We were sitting around a conference table in the personnel department – none of the grandeur of the Foreign Office reception rooms, no busts or mosaics, no murals of natives paying smiling tribute to the empress. A pair of photos hung on the wall, some of our people glad-handing local dignitaries somewhere, and I became transfixed with deciphering where they were. Caracas, I decided. Caracas or Bogotá.

'They took three hours to deliberate,' I tell her. 'Though one suspects it might well have been quicker if they hadn't broken for lunch. Gross misconduct. *Finita la commedia.*'

*

Olesya sighs and rocks back her head. Her throat: along with her eyes, her throat. They are not the features a man might be expected to prize or recall in a young woman, but there we are. I remember reading at school about Mary, Queen of Scots, how her poor, pale neck was almost translucent, how the red wine was visible in her gullet as she swallowed it.

I saw this little one, that one you bring to me. Very pretty picture.

'I didn't know you suffered like this,' she says. 'I'm sorry.'

A breeze delivers the aromas of mown grass and marijuana. She does not know the half of it, not yet.

'My daughter,' I say. 'Do you remember me mentioning my daughter Nancy?'

'You spoke about her, yes. The swimmer.'

'She's gone.' My mouth is dry. Count to ten, my mother used to say. 'No, no, she's alive. But I've lost her.'

'What does it mean, "lost"? For your child.'

'It means she won't speak to me. It means – how can I put it? It's like an amputation, that's the closest analogy. A missing limb.'

Olesya moans in what seems to be sincere sympathy. Odd that, the first time I try to articulate these feelings, it is to share them with the person responsible. 'The irony was, at first Cynthia believed me – Cynthia, my wife. But after the office suspended me, she changed her mind, and Nancy took her side.'

No, I don't need to hear it from you. Berating me down the line from school. *I don't need to hear anything from you. Never. Again.*

Never never never never never.

'I didn't say this about you.' She swallows. 'It's the truth.'

'You know, one expects to grow apart from one's child – no more bath times, no more sitting in my lap, the normal kind of separation. But not this. For a while she sent me the odd card, Christmas and so on.' *From Nancy.* 'And Cynthia deigned to help – emails, cursory updates – but after a few years she said, "You're both supposed to be grown-ups, you can work it out between you."'

In the summer, as a surprise after her exams, I was going to fly home and take Nancy to Paris. I was going to teach her to drive. When she was little, I remember, she would sit on my lap and steer.

'But you didn't work it out? With your daughter.'

'I tried. Cynthia moved up to Norfolk – after the divorce – she had always wanted to live near the coast, she claimed, though frankly I don't remember her ever saying so. She retrained, as a counsellor of some sort, and she met – she's living with a man. An antiques dealer, apparently.'

Living in sin – that was her mother's verdict when we first lived together. We had tried to dissemble, and if her old lady phoned, and I answered, I would improvise an excuse – *Just visiting, Passing through, Helping to fix the boiler* – all the while shushing Cynthia's giggles. When I proposed, on a coastal path in Devon, she held my cheek in her palm. I was clean-shaven then.

'I drove up, more than once, but Nancy wouldn't come out of the house. I slept in my car at the end of the driveway. And Cynthia and I, for all of our ... ups and downs, we had twenty years of marriage, twenty years of memories. ... I don't expect you to understand.'

Briefly I cover my eyes. Above us, a plane whines towards its runway.

'Don't you have someone else here? From your family.'

'At the beginning there was my father. I moved in with him while I tried to straighten things out. Rock bottom, really, to be back there at my age, but in a funny way it was a consolation. My mother had always been my point of contact, and later Nancy was the focus whenever we went down.'

He and I had conversed in a kind of well-meaning semaphore. *I'm fine, are you fine? Good.* Now we went to the cricket together, we drank two bottles of rosé on the Isle of Wight. He was tactful enough not to dwell on Kiev. With my mother, it would have been a different story.

'He had a good innings, but ...' I blink, hard. 'Fortunate that I could be there, really. At the end. That's what people said.'

Her hand motions towards me. 'I'm sorry for this loss.'

I raise an eyebrow to acknowledge the condolence. In truth, neither he nor I was prepared for the indecent intimacy of it all. At the funeral, as we were approaching the grave – it was raining – the rite suddenly felt like an ambush, an outrage, such that I had an urge to call the police.

As I say, it was as if it were happening to someone else. He barely left any money.

'After that, I rented a little flat, out in the suburbs, bit north of here. Not much, but sufficient for my purposes. I did some consulting for investors. I wrote a pamphlet.' *The Competition for Influence in Eurasia: Perspectives from the Black Sea.* 'It didn't last, though – it was as if, somewhere, a board had convened and passed a resolution that I was *persona non grata*. Not surprising, I suppose, considering the rubbish on the internet.'

'My parents are still living, glory to God. But what – if it is not a secret – what are you doing now? For money.'

'I don't have secrets anymore,' I tell her. After all, a secret can only begin, secrecy only obtains, when there is someone else to care. 'I drive, sometimes, these days. Topping up the savings till I take my pension. Different taxi apps, you know. Therapeutic, in a way. Like my swimming.'

'It's not so bad,' she says. 'You can live.'

I pass over my grimmest times, on my own, gin rather than rosé. I clear my throat. *The chair will now sum up.* 'So I hope it was worth it, Olesya. I hope you're satisfied, whatever it was that you got.'

Technical question.

'Whatever I got? Come with me,' she enjoins, rising from the bench and striding across the park. 'Come on.'

Nervously she drops her keys on the doorstep, bends to retrieve them and, for a moment, stays in her crouch, like a hedgehog balled to defend itself. Weeds hustle through the cracks in the forecourt of the pebbledash house. She leaves the front door ajar. 'Come in then, Simon,' she calls from inside. 'Come up.'

We will not be defeated!

Quietly, like a thief, I close the door behind us. Ahead of me, in the kitchen at the end of a stubby hallway, spray from the hobs is brownly visible on the wall above the stove. The house smells of beer, drains and disinfectant.

She reaches the first-floor landing as I begin to mount the stairs. The carpet on the steps is a patchwork of stains, the wallpaper coming away at the joins. A bare, low-watt bulb dangles from the ceiling. I count four doors – one of them, across from hers, opening onto a bathroom. I glimpse myself in a mottled mirror, with that momentarily delayed shock of recognition that comes upon one in late middle age and which, in my experience, one never outgrows. *That man is me.*

'In here.'

At the threshold of the bedroom I collide with a woman, not Olesya, younger, pink-cheeked, blond, wearing black Lycra leggings and a T-shirt. She frowns as she edges past me.

'This is Polly,' Olesya says, reappearing in the doorway. 'She may wait in the kitchen.'

'Thank you so much.'

'No guests overnight,' Polly says. 'It's rules.'

'Of course not.' I feel the colour rising in my cheeks. 'No question.'

Polly appraises me from the top step, with – I think – a smirk. Is it the fact of a man in Olesya's room, or this particular man, that she finds entertaining? After all, here I stand in my dowdy clothes, nowhere else to be on this weekday afternoon. She cannot know that I could-have-should-have-would-have been an ambassador.

It is always a useful exercise, is it not, to see oneself through an interlocutor's eyes? To the extent we can. Another lesson of my truncated career.

'It's fine,' Olesya says, vanishing into her room. Polly clomps down the stairs. 'She comes with her boyfriend after her shifts, they make me wait in the kitchen too.'

I hover at the threshold, like a TV policeman wary of an assailant. She is sitting on the edge of one of the two beds. The other, on the boxy room's opposite wall, is unmade, the disarranged sheets entwined with an institutional khaki blanket.

'Please,' she says, indicating the second bed.

How improper this might appear, I reflect – what hay they might make with this scenario – before I remember that, of course, how this looks no longer matters to anybody.

Bad optics, the ambassador would have said. Did say.

As instructed, I sit, shifting along the mattress so that we are arranged at a diagonal. The springs squeak. She takes off her boots and crosses her legs in a lotus position on the bed.

'The advert in the shop window said "private room",' she gripes, plugging in her phone. 'But it's cheap.'

Were they altogether wrong about Olesya and me? At the time I was aghast to be included among those colleagues – ex-colleagues – who prey on nubile locals, a minimum of one in every embassy, in my experience. But might my feelings have been more complex than I allowed, a protective urge contaminated with something baser? That sort of discrimination is hard to make among feelings as they are experienced, let alone in retrospect. Suspicion might only be natural, for Polly as it was for the office. It was natural for Cynthia, after what happened in Israel.

Why were you in that bar with her anyway? she wanted to know.

I was helping her friend – there was a fellowship in America—
Is that what they call it these days?
Darling, don't, it's hard enough for Nancy—
Don't bring her into it. Don't you dare bring her into it.

Her mouth bent into a new shape, like the mouth of the horse in the Picasso painting.

You know, you make me sick.

People say things they don't mean in these situations. And things they do mean.

You make me sick.

71

I do not mention the farrago in Israel to Olesya. It might come as a surprise, I expect, the association of the likes of me with desire, the news of our lustful old bodies.

'You said you hoped what I get is worth it. This is what I get. Take a look, please.'

I look. Against the far wall stands a set of plywood shelves, in front of which is a drying rack (white blouses, underwear, a blue dress). In the corner above Olesya's pillow, a patch of ceiling bulges rottenly. The window gives a view of the garden, or rather of the prefabricated cabin installed over what was once a garden, only one weedy border and an untrimmed hedge remaining. Above the cabin the view is interrupted, in the middle distance, by a tower block and a gasworks.

'This isn't what I thought.' Of all the lives I have imagined for her, in the past twelve years and in the last few hours, none resembled this one. 'I don't understand what you're doing here.'

Above her bed she has pinned up a picture of her brother, older but recognisable, making a V-sign in front of a barricade of tyres, a cigarette in his other hand. Andriy. He is smiling.

'People like me,' she says, 'we are not the ones who do such things, the things in the newspapers. We are not the carnivores. Perhaps you are not such a person as well. We are people who things are done to – object, not subject, I remember from my language class.'

'Olesya, with the greatest respect, I don't understand what you're talking about.'

'I am saying, it wasn't me who made this trouble for you. It wasn't your fault, but it wasn't my fault also.'

'But you were there. You were the only person there.'

'Was I?'

72

'Don't play games with me.'

The sweat ripples across my skin as I lean back against the wall. I have a sudden recollection of her in the embassy, sitting like this, just like this, legs crossed.

'Don't you see?' Abruptly, she rises and touches me, her palm on my cheek, on the bare skin between my beard and my eye. Her fingers are wonderfully cold.

'See what, exactly?'

'Whose house do you think that was today? On the river. As if I may know someone else with such a house. Come on, Simon – it was you who introduced us.'

4. The straw

AFTER A FEW minutes on his own, tapping his fingers on the tabletop, he swivelled in his seat to look for her. She was leaning on the bar, issuing instructions to the bartender, the contours of her body emphasised by her tiptoed stretch, her hair swept to one side of her neck. She returned to the table with a crowded tray, setting it down with a clatter in front of him.

'No, really,' Simon said. He checked his watch again. 'I'm not sure ... I shouldn't.'

She set out the glasses. 'They forgot our matches.'

Simon surveyed the room as she returned to the bar. A few of the customers sported orange memorabilia but most wore unadorned office clothes: men in grey suits who had discarded their ties; laughing women perched on high stools, winter coats draped over their seats. Jefferson Airplane wailed from the sound system. Simon's BlackBerry had lost its signal. He undid the top button of his shirt.

Olesya came back with the matches. 'Okay then,' she said. 'You never did this?'

74

'Never, I'm afraid. Wasted youth, I suppose.'

'It's very easy. Watch.'

She struck a match and ignited the liquid in one of the glasses, smiling across at him like an encouraging nurse. A blue flame shimmered on the Sambuca. She flipped the glass over and onto another one.

'You see,' she said. 'Gas is trapped.'

Don't you want somebody to love?

Nimbly she pulled the vapour-filled glass onto the table; beneath it was a paper napkin, plus a plastic straw that she had poked through the napkin and (now) beneath the rim and into the gas. She downed the warm liquor, grimacing only slightly, and inclined her face to suck the straw.

You better find somebody to love.

She puckered her lips around the plastic, closing her eyes as she sucked. When they opened they were watery; she blew out her cheeks and wiped her mouth with her sleeve. Her hair fell across her face.

Simon looked around. Two of the three men at a nearby table were watching them. One of them raised his beer glass in mock homage.

'Now you,' Olesya said. 'You must.' Her voice was hoarse.

'Perhaps I'd better not.' He glanced at the beer-drinkers. The third man at the table, red-faced and crew-cut, had turned to observe them, too. 'I'm on duty, you know. In a way.'

'Come on,' Olesya said. 'I show you.'

He squinted at his watch. 'Oh, all right then. Can't do any harm.'

She had emailed that afternoon to say that there was something she would like to ask him. Jacqui had intended to go with him, but the ambassador asked her to draft some remarks for a European round table.

'Her wish is my command,' Jacqui told Simon. 'I'll meet you and the girl there when I escape. To build the relationship, you know.'

'No need, really.'

'I'll see you there.'

Olesya had suggested the venue and Simon followed her directions. He had plunged into the labyrinth of passageways beneath Independence Square, where, to a soundtrack of busking teenage rockers and elderly accordionists, old women begged alongside disabled veterans, maimed in Afghanistan for a motherland that no longer existed. A man with no legs squatted alongside a wolfish dog; as Simon dropped a ten-*hryvnia* note into the man's hat the dog pressed its belly to the floor, making itself as harmless as possible. Subterranean kiosks sold underwear, DVDs, fake fur, aromatic *pyrizhky*. A portrait artist peddled hagiographic sketches of the politician with the braid.

He ascended to street level and found the unmarked door in an archway off Khreshchatyk, identifiable, up close, by the vibration of the music within. The bar was in a dimly lit cellar at the bottom of a spiral staircase. With its worn floorboards and exposed heating pipes, it had suffered the kind of dereliction that had aged into fashion. Olesya was waiting for him, drinkless and alone.

Her request was not on her own behalf, she told him. The problem had arisen because of a *temnyk*.

'You know what this thing is, a *temnyk*?'

'We do, yes. We've raised the issue several times, but the government stubbornly denies that they exist.'

Temnyky were covert edicts from the presidential adminis-tration that told the TV stations what they were to cover and how, and, conversely, which events they must ignore. Along with *titushky* – squadrons of plain-clothes, paid-for thugs, sent to intimidate and rough up protesters – *temnyky* were among the regime's habitual tools. *Temnyky* and *titushky*: the misleadingly cutesy lexicon of the two-bit authoritarian.

Olesya's asthmatic comrade from the march, Yaryna, worked for one of the state-run TV channels. Or, she used to. Yaryna had watched the sign-language interpreter's revolt – when, live on air, the interpreter had told her viewers that the official news was all lies, that she was sorry for her part in it, that they mustn't believe a word – and decided that she, too, would no longer comply with *temnyky*. She had said so and been fired on the spot. She was given to understand that her tax affairs were likely to be investigated, as were her father's.

'May you do something for her?' Olesya asked in the bar. 'You said, after our march, if there is anything you may do … Here is something. Not for myself. Speak to your friend Kovrin, he has his TV stations. Recommend her to foreign press.'

'He's not my friend. On the contrary. A figure like him – one doesn't want to be beholden, I'm afraid. To owe him any favours. But maybe there is something else.' Simon stroked his beard. 'Let me ask Jacqui.'

'She deserves something, really. She comes from Dnipro-petrovsk, in the south, close to the metal factories, pipes, their air full of chemicals. Mostly her family supports the govern-ment. And her health, you saw it – many times I said, the square is not for you, this cold, work in the museum, stay there, it's enough. But she comes. For her medicine, she needs money. She needs her job.'

'Well, perhaps we can make an introduction.'

'We thank you.'

'Don't mention it.' He glanced at his watch. 'But no promises, I'm afraid. All rather up in the air at the moment, as you know. By no means clear who's on top.'

'Who is, in your opinion?' Olesya said. 'Who will be?'

Rumour was queen of Kiev. She had grown grander in her prophecies and scope. No longer predicting drunken miners, busloads of *titushky* or released convicts, rumour was anticipating war. War with Russia, civil war, coups, sabotage, states of emergency. Already, rumour maintained, Russian *spetsnaz* had been secreted in position, ready to open fire if the order came down from Moscow. Each whisper shot across the city in a microsecond, quickly superseded by the next.

'Difficult to say,' Simon confessed. 'Evidently the government was hoping you would have all gone home by now. Meanwhile, there's the other struggle, inside the machine – between the people who want to make a deal, you know, give you a new election in return for immunity, assurances about keeping their assets, and, on the other hand, the hardliners who want to fight.'

'Which faction is Kovrin?'

He winced. 'I am not altogether sure. He talks tough but ... he might be persuadable.'

With rules of the game, I can accept.

'Does he matter still?'

'Yes, quite possibly he does. He has the old president's ear, that's why we brought him to the square in the first place. The

Supreme Court … I'm not sure we can count on the court, I'm afraid.'

She looked down at her hands. On the sound system, Soviet chanson gave way to American rock.

'Perhaps we ought—'

'Wait,' Olesya had said, setting off for the bar. 'Surprise.'

'I show you,' she repeated. Her cheeks were flushed, the colour seeping down her neck. In their deep sockets her eyes shone.

Simon hesitated. It was seven o'clock. He was not expected at the embassy that evening. On reflection, he had no reason to hurry home.

He glanced around the bar again. A few of the drinkers had begun to dance in a space between the tables, two young women and a rhythmless man. No one there knew him. Anonymity was a kind of freedom too.

'It looks rather fiddly,' he ventured. 'For an oaf like me.'

'Like this,' Olesya said. She poked a straw through a napkin and arranged the glasses. Sambuca dribbled onto her hand; she licked it off. She struck another match, set the liquor alight, flipped the glass and pushed the contraption across the table. Her nails were bitten down to the flesh, blue veins visible beneath the skin of her wrist. Simon reached for the straw.

'Drink first,' she told him.

He checked his watch for the last time: Jacqui was half an hour late. He nodded.

She separated the glasses and he drank the warm liquid, wiping his mouth with the back of his hand.

'Now finish it,' she told him.

He lowered his head, fiddled the straw between his lips and inhaled the liquoricey gas.

'I think,' Olesya said, 'we deserve it. For our morale.'

Simon puffed out his cheeks like a weightlifter before a snatch. His eyes bulged. 'That,' he gasped, 'is an important consideration.'

He inquired after Andriy, meaning only his whereabouts that evening, but she answered about all of him, her worries about her brother spilling out. They couldn't muster the bribe required to get him into university too, she explained: Andriy's school grades had been worse than hers, meaning the price was unaffordably high.

'It's justice, no?' Her throat was furred by the liquor. 'Better grades means you still pay their bribe, but you pay less. It's better rules than for traffic police. Speed makes no difference for police – speed of the car. Same price. Nowadays people slow down, wind their window, put out their money, pay without stopping. Better than for hospitals also. In hospitals, more sick you will be, more you must pay. Pay or die.' She wasn't smiling. 'Ask Yaryna.'

They couldn't afford to pay off the recruiting officer either, and so Andriy had gone to the army. Conscription; two years. They had worried that he might be sent to Iraq: the regime had been busted for selling arms to Saddam and was making up for it with the Americans. They didn't send him, but they ground him down. There was no hot water in the barracks and no heating, Olesya said, and in the winter the boys burned whatever they could find to keep warm. They washed once a week in the *banya*. They lived on *kasha* and gruel. The officers hired them out to work on building sites for gangsters – the gangsters paid for their fuel, and that was the only time the conscripts ever used their trucks, she told Simon, to build the gangster palaces. Andriy had to clean the brigade's toilets. He was beaten. He was hungry. He was cold.

'When he came home, he was different. Still Andriy, my brother. But quiet. He stays in his room, playing on his computer. Not interested in girls, not interested in work. Only this year, with our campaign, he wakes up again. Like a butterfly. He came to meetings at my university. He came with me to Kiev on election day, before they saw the flow of people and started to stop our trains. You know, when he was born, he came early '

'Premature.'

'Yes, and always, always, my mother worries for him. When we leave to Kiev, she makes me promise I will take care for him. At night he sleeps in a tent, but she does not know it, thanks to God.'

'It seems to me,' Simon said, 'that your brother Andriy is something of a radical. The other day, before your march – before the roses – his patience seemed to be wearing thin Fighting talk, you know. Slightly concerning.'

'He is angry, it's true. Because of the army, how they broke him, and because he thinks this is our only chance for something better. From a small boy he has a temper, shouting, hitting walls, but after he is sorry, he comes to our bedroom and he cries. I stroke his hair.'

She had brought water from the bar, as well as the liquor, and they sipped it. He offered to speak Russian but she said she preferred English.

'And you? You went from university to the hotel, is that right?'

Now the sound system was playing power ballads. The man on the improvised dance floor was slow-dancing with one of the women. Her friend smoked a cigarette as she observed their clinch from a stool.

'Last summer, I graduated. But already before, I was working in reception. Guests are Germans, some Americans. Some Russians. Polish. Some waitressing also. Our managers are honest people, I was lucky, there was no bribe to pay to get my job.'

'Did you enjoy it? Your work.'

'You know, I remember, I asked my grandmother one time about her job. She worked in a factory, since Khrushchev times, fifties. Not in Ivano-Frankivsk, in Ternopil. Lighting – lamps, electrics. She said, about her work, it was "hot in summer, cold in winter". So, that is how it was for me. Normal. Not to speak about work – not to think about it, even, to hold it separate – it keeps you strong.'

'Quite,' Simon said. 'I suppose, in that respect, I've been rather fortunate – we had a few years in America, now here, not a bad run at all. No virtue of my own, really, just an accident of birth.' He paused. 'What will you do when this is over? Back to the hotel?'

'I hope, no. Maybe I will help in television, like Yaryna. Or, after we win, maybe I will work for our new government – foreign relations, like you.' She sipped her water. 'You understand, the world knows nothing about my country. Chernobyl, something about our Great Patriotic War, terrible things only. Famine, sometimes, some people know. Most people, until now, they don't know even that it *is* a real country. I mean, independent country.'

'I know precisely what you mean.' Simon took off his jacket and rolled his sleeves up to his elbows; the sparse hair on his arms was stark against his pink skin. The cigarette smoke stung his eyes. 'There was a journalist at the embassy today, one of ours, the worst kind. Exactly as you say, he might have been on the moon.'

Dorian Thompson had been peeved to find, on arrival at the embassy, that his interlocutor was to be Simon rather than the ambassador. Beneath his station, he evidently felt, disdain he had made no effort to conceal.

'So it's a racial conflict, then?' He flipped over Simon's business card as if he were playing tiddlywinks.

'With the greatest respect,' Simon said, 'I don't think race has anything to do with it.'

'I think perhaps Dorian means cultural,' Jacqui interjected. 'Cultural and linguistic.'

'That's it. Is that the kind of conflict it is? The Russian side and ... the other lot.' Thompson checked his phone.

'If you'll forgive me, I don't think "conflict" is the word to use. It's a political crisis, and it needs a political solution.'

'What Simon is saying is that we have faith in the institutions.'

'I think I can make myself understood.'

'That wasn't what—'

'Thank you, Jacqui.'

'I was only trying to help.' She flushed. Thompson had run out of questions before the coffee arrived; the men did not shake hands when he left. Jacqui had steered him out of the embassy, her hand elevated behind his back but not touching him.

'Frankly speaking,' Olesya said to Simon, 'it is not their fault.' She rolled an empty glass between her palms. 'It is our fault, our government. The face they show to the world. This man they want for president now, on television he uses words from prison. He was in prison before, himself. My grandmother said they used bandits like this in Soviet times – the Kremlin made them little bosses. An honest man, nobody needs, an honest man may say no. But bandits will do anything you want.'

She put down the glass and laid her hands flat on the table. 'What about one more drink?'

Simon looked down at his own hands, resting close to hers, his forearms bare where hers were encased in the sleeves of her turtleneck. He was tired. He was a diplomat. It was cold outside. He was lonely.

'Allow me,' he said.

He went to the bar and came back with the bottle.

'Let me see if I can remember.'

'Yaryna and me,' she told him as he poured, 'we learn this trick at university.'

'Interesting curriculum.'

He set her glass alight, then his. The table resembled a debauched science experiment. They drank their shots in synchrony, bumping heads when they leaned forward to inhale the fumes. Simon winced and closed his eyes. When he opened them, two of the beer-drinkers were applauding.

She told him about her grandmother, the woman from the lamp factory. Yes, she was still living, Olesya confirmed. The old lady had been born in the same region as her, only it was in another country then, before the Soviets came. She was an expert gatherer of mushrooms; once she let slip that she had eaten shoe leather and tree bark during the war. Every time, when the news bulletin came on the television, she would say that it was all lies. She had warned Olesya, when she began to be involved in politics, that it was safest never to volunteer for anything. This was one of her survival rules. Don't believe the news. Accept no favours from anyone who might, in return, ask for something you would not want to give. And never volunteer.

'But she does not understand,' Olesya said. 'To volunteer freely, it is different. For her, life is good – life is enough – if it is better than the worst.'

'Perfectly understandable,' Simon said. 'Woman of her generation. The things they went through.'

He loosened his tie so that the knot hung raggedly on his chest. The orange anthem boomed from the speakers. *We will not be defeated!* Some of the drinkers cheered.

'In her house – it's a traditional cottage, wooden, painted blue and white – in her house she has a washing machine. But no pipes, no water. She uses it for her cupboard. It's true.'

The second drink was the mistake; after that, the third was inevitable. They lit the Sambuca but dispensed with the straws and the gas.

'To victory!' she said. They clinked.

'To the friendship of peoples!' he reciprocated, the old Soviet standard. The liquid bit his throat.

She asked about America. They were there in the nineties, he told her, war was blazing in the Balkans, but they seemed comparatively innocent times, and regardless, he said, they had been happy. Nancy was little and living with them and they saw each other every day.

'There was one occasion,' Simon said, 'she was at the local swimming pool, nine years old. No, eight. Not a strong swimmer. The lifeguard, she climbed down from her chair and said Nancy couldn't go in unless she could do a whole length. By herself, you know. And she wanted to swim, she badly wanted to.' He pinched the bridge of his nose. 'Really, I don't know why I'm telling you this.'

'It's okay,' Olesya said. 'Tell it.' She patted his hand.

'So she pushes herself off the end, she's doggy-paddling and stretching her neck, you know, like an elderly woman protecting her hairdo, and it was a big pool, and she tired, and the lifeguard turned towards us and sort of smiled, you know, like this' – he flinched one side of his mouth – 'so I, you know, jumped in.' He beamed at the memory. 'Shorts still on, socks. Swam out to her in the middle, everybody watching me, but didn't touch her. Couldn't. Just told her, you know, "You can do it, popsicle." She looked at me sort of newly. When she finished she hugged me in the water, thin and cold in her purple bathing suit. Told me I was the best daddy in the world. But, you know, when I remember it, that afternoon, part of it is the feeling of being so close to her and not being able to reach her. I shouldn't be telling you this, I'm sorry.'

She patted him once more. 'She is lucky. A lucky girl to have you.'

He said, 'Like a premonition.' Briefly he hung his head.

'Really, it's okay,' Olesya repeated. 'To watch time go past like this, with children, it's normal.'

He drained his glass. 'She's at school now, in England. Boarding school, you know. Do you know? University soon, like you. She looks ... you remind ... younger than you, of course.'

He did not dwell on their posting in Tel Aviv. He poured himself another drink, filling his glass to the brim. Olesya put a hand over hers when he moved to replenish it. He undid his tie and shoved it into his trouser pocket; the end snaked out like a schoolboy's. The neck of his vest showed at his open collar.

'Your wife,' Olesya said. 'She is here, in Kiev?'

'My wife,' Simon said. 'My wife … In a manner of speaking.' He stared vacantly at the paraphernalia on the table. 'I mean to say, yes, she's here. Absolutely. Cynthia. She has – she's doing – a project on icons. Fascinating, the history. A trooper.'

He slid his hand towards Olesya's. On the way his fingers knocked over a glass, the water cascading from the table and soaking one of his thighs.

'So sorry,' she said. 'Let me – I get something.'

'It's nothing,' Simon said. 'Absolutely not your fault.'

She fetched a roll of paper towel from the bar, kneeling beside him on the worn floorboards to mop the puddle at his feet. She considered but did not touch the damp patch on his trousers; he looked down at the top of her head and the arm briskly scrubbing a circle on the stained floor. A seam of black Lycra was visible between her jeans and her sweater.

She stood, wiped the edge of the table and balled the towels amid the detritus of their drinks. The bottle was still half full.

'Don't mention it. Please.'

'So sorry.'

The bar was crowded now and they had to raise their voices to be heard.

'It's a funny business, though,' Simon said. 'Mine is. Rather gruelling for the wives – the spouses, I mean, these days. Dragged around, pillar to post, a long way from home. One ought to be understanding, I know, but sometimes, the separate lives ...'

'Yes,' Olesya agreed, carefully, as if assessing the evening's possible trajectories. She redirected their conversation. 'My mother, she feels like this for Andriy and me. That we are too far away from her.'

'Naturally. Febrile times. Uncertain. A mother.'

'She told me, in Mukachevo yesterday, *titushky* came to their town square, where protesters were, our side. They bring clubs, knives, and police only watch them. She says you may still see the blood. It starts. Not here, not in Kiev, where the newspapers are, television cameras, where you are, the foreigners, but in other places.'

'We heard about that. Nasty.'

'Here they say they brought in troops from outside – from Crimea, from Russia – because our city men, they won't shoot us. Is it true?'

This was part of rumour's power – a residue of credence remained even if the whispers were unproven. Because the rumours had once been believed, they entered the realm of the possible. Because they were possible, in a sense the treachery or atrocity had happened, only metaphysically, in the imagination. They carried almost the same weight as events that happened in fact. They blurred: the things that happened and the things that might have.

The roof there, you see – no, not here, that one, on top of shops.

'I've. ... We've ... No wish to cause alarm,' Simon said. 'Not productive, in our view. But there's a lot of it about, I know. Highest levels – even Tina Vlasych ... Forgive me, I shouldn't talk about it.'

'What about her?'

'This morning ... But I shouldn't.'

'What did she say?'

Vlasych had been at the embassy too, right after Thompson, in a shoulder-padded jacket like a character from an eighties soap. The finale is coming, she had told them. They didn't know how long they could keep their people on the square in the cold, though the good news was, their opponents in the government didn't know either. Neither did the Russians who were backing them, even with their apparatchiks on the ground, the grizzled aficionados of slander and bewilderment whom the Kremlin had sent over on loan.

She wanted sanctions, pronto: against the government candidate; against the outgoing president, who had just flown back from Moscow; against the oligarchs. 'Because it all costs money, right? The TV news, the doctors who said the poisoning was a case of bad sushi. You know, before the election, whenever we had a rally, we'd get there to find there was a circus on the same spot. I mean, a real circus. Horse shit. Camel shit. Elephant shit! They've got a sense of humour, you've got to give them that.'

'Rolling in the aisles,' Simon said. 'No doubt.'

'And *their* rallies? Nobody goes to them unless they're paid.' She rubbed her thumb and forefinger together. 'You know how they claim that we're paying our guys? Always accuse your opponent of whatever scam you're working yourself – that's the basic MO.'

The diplomats told her they were waiting for the Supreme Court to rule. They said they had called on the police to respect the right of peaceful protest.

Vlasych slapped her palm down on the table, her rings cracking on the surface. 'Do you have any idea,' she had said, 'the pressure they are putting on those guys? The judges, I mean. The death threats! Half of them have sent their children out of the country. And the police? The po-lice? Do you know how much those officers paid for their positions? Thirty thousand dollars, fifty thousand. They've got to keep the jobs long enough to recoup their investments. And they know that if we win, they won't. Period.'

She slapped the table again, more softly. This time her rings made a dead thud. 'You know,' she said, 'what they're angling for now? They want to disqualify the candidates, ours and theirs. They'll run that suit from the central bank instead.'

'If I may,' Simon asked, 'where does that intelligence come from? About the plan for a rerun.'

'Let one just say,' Vlasych replied, affecting an English accent, 'one has one's sources. Close to the president, let's put it that way.' She looked out of the embassy window. 'I had a nice little life in Westchester. Cabin in the mountains, boat on the lake, little jetty. Real estate law, mostly. A nice, easy life. But you grow up on these stories, you know, the old country – terrible stories, a lot of them, but there's also the romance of it, the hope ... So I get here and I find the Kremlin's playing hardball and you guys are playing – what do you call it, with the sticks?'

'Croquet, I believe.'

'I'll say this for Moscow, at least they're ponying up – propaganda 24/7, the slush fund to buy off the army. But you guys ... You think this is where all of this bullshit ends? The dirty money and the rest of it. Because I'm warning you, it won't.'

Simon and the others had nodded politely. 'This is it,' she had said at the door. 'Show time.'

*

'Show time,' Simon mumbled in the bar. 'That's what they say. I shouldn't, I'm sorry ...'

'So it's true?' Olesya said. 'It means it's true. About the soldiers from outside.'

'In confidence,' Simon said, 'in confidence, I ... We don't know.' Her face fell. 'So sorry ... terribly opaque situation ... awfully ... forgive me ... I don't want to say more than ... more than ...'

'It's clear.' She forced a smile. 'But you will tell me, please? When you know something.'

'If I can, by all means. Entirely understandable.'

He poured himself another drink, crashing the bottle down on the table. From the foot of the stairs, Jacqui and Iain turned towards the bang. Their view was obscured by the dancers, but when the bodies parted, they spotted Simon. Simon and Olesya.

They squeezed towards the table through the crush. Simon saw them approaching, and waved, and went back to his conversation, untroubled.

'So sorry I'm late,' Jacqui said, appraising the bottle of Sambuca, the scrunched-up paper towels, the multiple glasses, the straws, the spillages. 'I brought Iain, he insisted.'

'Not at all,' Simon said. 'Mention it.' He stood up, leaning too heavily on the table so that it almost overbalanced.

Iain reached out to right it. He sighed and shook his head. 'Good lad,' he said softly as he gripped Simon's shoulder. 'Be a good lad.'

Jacqui's eyes were drawn to the damp patch on Simon's trousers. He registered her attention and covered the area with a hand. She took in his rolled-up sleeves, the tie dangling from his pocket, her inventory veering upwards to his open shirt and vest. Above the line of his beard, a maze of blood vessels was traced on his cheeks.

She turned to Olesya. 'Miss Zarchenko, good evening.'

'Yes,' Olesya said. She was more composed than Simon, but her cheeks were still flushed and her eyes glistening. She stood up. 'It's me.'

'Good lad,' Iain repeated. 'Let's be having you then.' He ignored Olesya and began to steer Simon to the door.

Simon wheeled back to the table for his jacket and coat. He reached for the bottle but Iain snatched it away. 'Not empty,' Simon said.

'Never mind now,' Iain said. 'It's empty enough.'

'My friend,' Olesya said, grasping Simon's wrist. 'Yaryna. You'll remember?'

'Naturally. One always ... Any friend of ... Jacqui will see to it.'

'See to what?' Jacqui said. 'Simon, see to what?'

'Your daughter,' Olesya said. 'She's lucky.'

'You're so kind,' Simon said. 'So very kind.'

'That'll do,' Iain said. He guided Simon up the spiral stairs and through the archway that opened onto Khreshchatyk. Jacqui followed silently. 'Good lad,' Iain murmured.

Inlaid in the ceiling of the arch was a Soviet-era mosaic of the night sky, the moon and stars picked out in white against an indigo background. Out on the road, in the real sky, no stars were visible.

iv. Fairy lights

A SECRET means power, as everybody knows, but power for who? With a single secret, it is clear, there can be more than one answer. Here, in this room, I know something Simon does not, a secret he badly wants, and so, although he followed me, though he is angry and has a right to be, between us, while I keep it, I have the power. Because I know what happened that night. On Independence Square.

At the same time, it matters who the secret touches. It matters who owns it. If you know the secret of an influential man, a rich man, a ruthless man, you are not powerful but the opposite. Such a secret is like a debt you cannot pay. To put it another way, between the torturer who wants the secret and the victim who hides it, where does the power lie? Who is the subject and who is the object?

'Kovrin,' Simon says. He breathes hard, like a caught fish. 'Are you saying that was Kovrin's house? When I saw you go in there, I gathered you were mixed up in something ... But not him.'

I nod, slowly.

'I didn't know he was in London.'

'Sometimes London, sometimes Paris or Capri. Sometimes, still, he goes to Kiev. When he must.'

'But you and he, you came from different worlds. And now the two of you are – what, exactly? Friends?'

'I wouldn't call it friends.'

His mouth is open, as when the caught fish stops breathing. His eyes stare over my shoulder, at the empty wall. For what he is thinking, he cannot look at me.

'You mean – between you and Kovrin, romantically, is there …'

You are kind, Kovrin said to me. *So kind. Will you be kind?*

'I would not call it romance, either.'

Simon makes a face like he has a pain in his liver. Always in this country, I have noticed, a person thinks his feelings are the most important thing, his own pain. The moon moves round the Earth, the Earth moves round the sun, but the whole universe moves round each person here. His wife, his daughter. Now this, as if his shock matters more than the shocking thing that happened to me.

'Is that … What were you doing there? By the river.'

'I was collecting my wages,' I say. 'No, not for that, all that is finished. For the cleaning, the housekeeper pays me. They need the money at home, this month we couldn't wait.'

'What cleaning? What are you talking about?'

'I clean their house. The Kovrins. Three times a week, more when they are there. I look after a girl, clean two more houses near the museums.'

'What girl?'

'An English girl. Not mine.'

'This isn't what I thought at all.'

Some of them want you to love the child, they feel better if you do. Some of them want no feelings, not yours, not the child's. Some of the men, they do not speak, they do not see you. Some, they look at you, they stand in the kitchen, drinking their coffee and looking, and it is better to go to another room.

'I did what I had to do. That's it.'

'And you're saying it was Kovrin – that winter – that Kovrin was behind it all?'

Did I think of Simon during these years? Of course I did. But he went back to London, he suffered nothing terrible, I thought it was not the end of his world. Or I chose to. Because, in any case, I could not help him.

You must never say, not tonight, not ever. Never tell anyone.

Later, if he came into my mind, I would try to push him away.

'Like I said, it wasn't me. As I tried to explain on the square.'

'Please,' he says, gripping Polly's blanket like he must hang on for his life. 'Tell me what happened.'

None of this is what he thinks, not bad against good, that was not the story. There is no pattern here, the game has no rules. Despite everything he has seen, America and the world, he does not understand this simple thing.

'Wait.' I never wanted to lie to him and I do not want to lie to him now. 'Wait and I will tell you.'

To Simon, I know, I was an icon, Lady Revolution. An angel. But, if one of us was naive that winter, I do not think that it was me. It was not the politicians on the stage who I believed in. It was the crowd – it was us. I knew someone was paying, for the food we served in the Lenin Museum, the lights, the big TV, whatever they gave the police, and I knew that, in the end, they would have to be paid back, same as ever. Still, on the square, with my friends all around like a party, or like in church, a party in church, I thought life would be better. Not perfect, but better. The lines between the people seemed to be fading out, the lines between what is possible and what is not, between now and the future. We could make it ourselves – the future – we could force it.

'He said he would help me,' I tell Simon. 'That spring, they called me. First it was Thibaut, he phoned and said "Wait". Then Kovrin came on. He would like to do something for me, I should come to his TV station. I was a risk for him, because of what I knew, a problem, and so – in his world – I owed him. I could not say no, do you see?'

'What risk? What had you done to him? Olesya.'

I smile. Not *to* him. *For.*

'So I went. My friend Yaryna, she was working there, they hired her after the revolution. He was different – Kovrin – like this was what he always wished for, free speech, free press. They gave me a job, booking guests, booking cars. We joked, me and Yaryna, that one day we will have our own show.'

Evening on the Square, I remember the name. We made up the theme tune – *dum, da da dum dum*. We sang it to each other in the mornings.

'It was the best time, I think, those few months, not only for me. There were no bribes, like they held their breaths, the bureaucrats, waiting to see what the new rules would be. Tourists were coming again – my mother was busy as a guide, Andriy was her driver. We had won, we thought. We were happy.'

In my head I can see Simon, in the car to Kovrin's, his hands in his lap like a child, knees together like a woman's. He was a big player, he thought then, a serious player. Like he could play against Kovrin.

'Thibaut,' he says. 'I remember him. Something off about him. Always smiling.'

I remember him too. *You must never say. Mr Kovrin will be most upset.* But now, here we are.

'He was not often in the office,' I continue. 'Kovrin. All his money is from the factories, the mines, he had the TV channels for politics. His toy. Then one day he comes and finds me, leans on my desk, taps his fingers. He tells me he has a suggestion, a "new concept". He says he has an apartment.'

'No doubt he does.'

'An empty apartment, he would like me to see it. When he had this idea for me, I cannot say. Anyway, I go. I must.'

Kovrin did not say anything then about the night in the revolution. He did not need to. What he knew about me – and more than that, what I knew about him – I think I understood that in the end there must be a price.

'Naturally you do.'

'The apartment is in Baseina Street, on the other side of Besarabsky market. I arrive and he is already there. Nobody with him, no guards. He lets me in.'

'I understand,' Simon says. Between the buttons on his shirt I see his pink belly, like a pig's. 'There is really no need.'

He does not understand. Also I think he wants to know, even if he does not say so. In the corner of this room, in the shadow like a hiding animal, there is sex. It is always here – even before I went to Kiev, I learned that. In that bar with

Simon, before his colleagues found us – the man and that woman – it was there, I knew it. I was not his angel, and I was not a saint.

'Kovrin shows me the apartment – it is in a courtyard, through a small gate – he shows it and says, no one is living here, would you like it? I ask him who pays, the lights, the gas. "Technical question," he says.'

No strings. Absolutely no strings.

'Rather too good to be true,' Simon says.

'A favour for him, that's what he tells me. Straight away he left the keys. I was living with my cousin still in the block on the Left Bank. Fifth floor, no elevator. I did not have much to move.'

Absolutely no strings.

Simon looks at me like a stranger. It is a surprise, what people may do, I agree – what I may do. It is news. Myself, I look back now on this woman, and I ask, who is she? At the same time, when I search for the place where I made the mistake, the time when I might have run, I cannot find it. I cannot see what else I should have done.

'I have to say, this is not how I remember you,' he says.

'In Kiev,' I say, 'they call it "sponsorship". Not ... something else. Like a kind of uncle.'

I went through a gate into the courtyard. In the trees there were fairy lights, they hung across the parking places that people argued for. In some of the apartments, like mine – Kovrin's – they had made a *remont*, everything was new, but in some of the others they had not, and there the old women sat on their balconies, eating sunflower seeds, watching.

'Some uncle.'

Every night when the sun goes down, the lights in the trees go on.

'But in the beginning it was true, what he said. He left. Then, after some time, he invites me to lunch. Then dinner in a restaurant. He was not careful about being seen with me. Why be careful, a man like him?'

You are very kind. Be kind.

'As I say, I think we can do without the gory details.'

'When finally the time came it seemed that it had already been decided. Like in a game of chess, when any move you make will end in the same way.'

I did not tell my mother, my father – my brother. I told them I was staying with a friend. Even Yaryna, I told her everything only later. She said nothing but she turned her face away. I knew what she thought, just as I see what Simon thinks now. I thought the same.

'I guess your opinion,' I say to him. 'And I hated it, every second, you could not know ... But I closed my eyes and found a way. He came once a month, he did not hurt me, I must say that. Then at last he stopped coming.'

Simon covers his eyes.

'It seemed to me that Kovrin's wife knew, Natalia. I saw her once in his office – I was there and she arrived, they were going to the opera, the new building that he paid for. I do not think she was surprised.'

Be kind.

'So instead he brought you here, is that right? To London.'

'Not then,' I say. 'He let me stay. At first. Probably there were other girls, other apartments. But at a certain point Kovrin decides *no*. So he sent Thibaut and he ... he was not nice with me.'

He thought – Thibaut – that he was like the squire of the lord, the baron's man, and so he was allowed, he had a right to me, as if I was meat from the baron's table. After I refused, and pushed him away, he smiled in the mirror in the entrance hall and fixed his tie. I see Thibaut's smile in the mirror.

'Well, I'm sorry to hear that,' Simon says. He wants to be tough, cruel even, but his anger is like make-up on an actor, his kindness shows through underneath. He strokes his beard.

'What the devil gives,' I say, 'he must always take back.'

It is all the same, I learned – when they want to save you, to be the hero, or when they want to have you. I was a detail, a supporting actress in their drama. The men who planned to hurt us on Independence Square, the men who sent me to the barricades with a rose, the man behind his mask who asked for my phone number. Afterwards, Kovrin. Then Thibaut. This man, now, here in my room, mourning for himself. They don't really see you at all.

He stands up from the bed. For a moment he gazes through the window at the blue sky the English love, and which they talk about, when it comes, as if it was theirs only. He looks at the photograph of Andriy, his mouth open as if he is remembering something. When he speaks, he says only that he would like a glass of water.

'Downstairs,' I tell him. I hear his careful steps, he is trying to be quiet. The way he sits, how he watches the door – he is in dark territory here. In this house, I should tell him, my room is the Ritz. In the cabin, they sleep in turns. Same bed, same sheets.

He sits back on the mattress. Water spills as he places his drink on the carpet – I can see the coffee stains inside the mug. The lemon smell of my cleaning work is in my nostrils, in my hair.

'Go on,' he says. 'I'm listening.'

'So, I quit the job. I thought that between me and Kovrin, it was over. That I had lived through it. Already, at that time, things in Kiev were starting to go bad. Vlasych – you remember Vlasych?' He nods. 'She was trying to sell meetings with our president, they made a tape of her, she ran away. The people that winter who told us, you are crazy, you are children, you are putting in bandits in place of bandits ... They were right, weren't they? They were right.'

My country is like a small character from the beginning of the movie. You forget him, he is mixed up with the others, but he comes back for the end. He knows something, he is a clue, and in the end you see that he mattered after all. The black money and the black PR that now are everywhere. The Moscow way.

Glory to you all!

'So, I moved back home, to my parents. My grandmother was living still, thanks to God. After some time I went back to my job at the hotel.'

'Quite a comedown from the big city, I imagine. The chic apartment.'

Despite everything, it is beautiful there. The fields like a quilt with the mountains behind them, in the villages each house has beehives in front, and a well, painted and colourful. The storks make nests. Walnut trees and wildflowers, old women with their headscarves, old men plough the fields with horses.

Beautiful and poor. And full of ghosts. I was fifteen, I was walking in the woods with my brother, giant oaks as in a fairy tale, and we found a stone, there were plants growing over it. A memorial – *To the slaughtered Soviet citizens* – and for the first time I understood, I perfectly understood, that in my home we walk on bones. In the towns where the prisons were, in the countryside. They cracked under my feet, I could hear them. Andriy took my arm.

'They were another peaceful time, those months. Work, home, some friends from university. I thought that I was free. A happy ending.'

'But he found you?'

'No – I found him.' I sigh. 'Over there, you may not simply choose your story – the news is not just for television, it comes into your life. The orange politicians fought each other, and when we had another election, the bandit candidate, Moscow's pet, became president after all. Soon the crooks in epaulettes started the raids – against the businesses, I mean, whoever had something valuable that they wanted – and they came for the hotel. They used the tax police, health inspectors. One morning there was a new manager, a small man with a shaved head and a leather jacket. He told me to go.'

'And you threw yourself on Kovrin's mercy?'

'Not yet. I found other work, waitressing, translation. But then, four years ago, the new protests came – against the bandit, all the corruption – and Andriy, my brother, he went back to Kiev with his army friends. He helped to work a catapult, I saw the photos, it looked like it should be in the Middle Ages, defending a castle from the Mongols. The boys tore up the cobblestones, they burnt tyres. He was there, on this road from the presidential administration, when they started shooting. The snipers.'

Bullets instead of roses, this time, and no one to stop it. They killed a hundred people before the bandit ran away. Simon looks again at the photograph.

'He wasn't—'

'He's okay, he's going to be okay. My mother takes care of him, he can walk. But nobody does anything for these hurt boys, for his medicines, only us. My father has a pension but it is nothing, like a tip in a restaurant for thirty years. Soon the war began with the Russians, and there were no jobs, no money. Yaryna went to Austria, she got married there and stayed. And I—'

'What? You what?'

'I phoned him, God help me. Kovrin. It was all I could think of.'

In my mind I see my finger on the phone. Dial, don't dial. Dial. Don't.

'He took you back?'

'She answered. His wife, Natalia. I told her I had trouble, I told about the time at her house, all those years ago, I was frightened, she embraced me. I said, "Do you remember?"'

'Very forgiving lady, by the sound of it.'

'I thought she would not help, but after three days she calls back. Probably she did not make a link to the moment in his office. Maybe Kovrin wanted to keep me close, who knows? "Come to London," she says, "we need a girl there, why don't you come? We need someone for the house, the children."'

With Kovrin, the past is like a switch that he may turn off. He flicks his switch and what happened between us in Baseina Street is covered in darkness. For him it is always today. Always now. He knows I will never tell her.

'Yes,' Simon says, 'he talked about his children. Bit sentimental, underneath it all.'

'His little princes,' I say. 'Little monsters.'

I think morals are like that for Kovrin also. They are there, he has them, I am certain that he does, but sometimes, when his morals make a problem for him, when he needs to, he flicks his switch and they are gone. Like a magician.

This is something else Simon does not understand. He wants the world to be made from good and evil, and it is not, it is money against the rest. He thinks that some are good and some are bad, but they are not, we are not, there are only people, and at different times they will do different things. So.

There is a knock on the door and Polly comes in. She goes to her washing, feels the dress is damp, she makes her angry face and pulls it from the rack. She stands between the beds, holding the dress, and tilts her head towards Simon.

'Please,' I say. 'She wants to change.'

He leaves the room and she drops her work clothes. She puts on the dress and I do her zip. Her hair is loose but she ties it with a band. There is a small tattoo on her neck, three blue stars. She works in the old people's home. She tells sad stories.

'Who is it?' Polly asks. I can hear him outside the door. He coughs. 'Is it from work?'

Simon is the first person I have brought here, a funny thing. When I do not answer she turns to face me. 'It's okay, with this man?'

'Yes,' I say. 'He's okay. He's from home.'

Polly wants to be a bookkeeper. Sometimes she snores, but often she is not here. The Ritz!

She leaves and he comes in again. He sits closer now. It is almost time, he can sense it. We are coming to the end, or rather the beginning. We are coming to Independence Square.

'You came to London,' he says. 'Go on then.'

'They got me a visa,' I tell him. 'Domestic servant. This house – he calls it his "river cottage" – he bought it already when the bandit was president. There were no rules then, no limits, and so he takes his family out, his money. I had a room at the top, like an old English maid. I could see the water.'

'Quite the ménage.'

'In London, I must say, he never ... he never came near me. Already I decided that if he tried, I would leave, I would scream. But he never did. In the evenings I took language classes, I walked along the river. I thought this might be a life.'

On the stairs there is a queue for the bathroom. Loud voices, different languages. In England, the nice people, they worry about trafficking, they imagine violence and chains, but for most of us, this is not the risk. Life is the risk here, just life. People think they are climbing up, but they find that they have fallen down. Like the end of communism – my father was a physicist and he worked in the dairy, I studied philology and I clean Kovrin's steam room. His cinema room, his panic room. Their separate bathrooms. Their separate bedrooms. You start at the bottom and say thank you.

'If I may,' he says, 'what are you doing here?' His eyes slide to the door and then the window with the cabin outside. 'In this house.'

'This is not the worst place, really it is not.'

I am a child of the Soviet Union, if only for my first years, and this helps me here, I think. No one had space then, we did not think of privacy.

'But why if they allowed you to stay—'

'Two winters ago, they say they do not need me, their boys are grown, *do svidaniya*. I think, for Kovrin, what I know about him is not so important anymore. So then I tell her everything – Natalia – all about Andriy, his leg, how at home, they live from what I send. I beg.'

'And what did she say?'

'She says I may clean for them still, I should find my own room but they will keep my visa. She touches my arm, and I thank her. Since then, this is my life.'

'You always looked out for him, as I recall – Andriy – even back then, on the square.'

'He's my brother, what else should I do?'

One summer, when we were children, we went to Crimea. All the resorts that had belonged to the *nomenklatura* had been taken by people who were suddenly rich. They built fences around them, but Andriy climbed over, into an orchard. He was ten, maybe eleven, he was already tall. I told him not to, but he did it. He came back with four apples, one for each of us, tied in his T-shirt. His smooth chest was bare.

Always together, that's what we said to each other. Red apples.

'I am sorry about your brother,' Simon says. He straightens his back. 'Truly I am. But that's enough. Tell me about that winter, about you and Kovrin and what you did to me. Now, please.'

I remember that night, everything about it, the night Simon's life turned, and mine also. On the hill, away from the crowd on the square, the snow had frozen to ice, black ice, invisible. I slipped and fell. *The church is near, but the way is icy*: my grandmother told me this proverb and that was how it felt. Outside the ministry I saw the policemen and I thought the army had already come, I was too late. My eyes were running from the cold, or I was crying, I cannot say. The guard comes from his hut, he says I am not on his list, and I perfectly understand that he will never let me in and I cannot stop the blood.

Up the hill, get up the hill, your friends are on the square. Your brother. You promised to look after him.

'All right,' I say. 'They said it was forbidden to tell, but it's time.'

'Who did you talk to? About what happened in the embassy.'
Do the good thing or do nothing.

'Thibaut,' I say. 'I talked to Thibaut, only him.'

That night I saw the woman, the one I met at the university. She opened the door of the small room, she made a face with her eyebrows, then she went away. Simon did not see her – not that night, not ever, he never saw her, that was how it seemed to me. As if she was invisible to him, a mouse. A ghost.

'But why Thibaut?'

'Because,' I say, 'it was Thibaut who sent me up to you from Independence Square. "Go to the embassy," he said. It was the only way. And so I came.'

He holds his head in his hands, his fingers locked together behind it. He bends his face to his knees, like you must do on an aeroplane when it will crash. I turn my face towards the ceiling, to the place where the water comes through in the rain.

'That isn't what you told me.'

'I know what I told you.'

'You mean the whole thing ... I thought I was helping you, but it was Thibaut and Kovrin all along?'

'I had no choice. Over and over, they warned not to say who sent me. Against them, what was I?'

I had no American Express, I had no British passport. What did I have? I had a mother and a father, and – still – my grandmother. All easy to find if I disobeyed and Kovrin decided to punish us. I had my brother on the square and nothing more. It was life, not an adventure, not a game. This is a feeling that Simon can never know. Then and later, it was life or death.

'Did you have to – was it really necessary – the part about you and me – that we—'

'That wasn't me, as I swore to you.' This is also the truth. 'I said nothing like this, to no one. So.'

My phone rings. It is the Wilsons, I see on the screen, the wife. *Yes*, I say to Mrs Wilson, *of course. Tomorrow is fine. Yes, five-thirty is fine. Kiss her for me.*

I hang up. 'Client,' I say. 'Babysitting.'

They hear your accent and they ask where you are from, or they make a guess, and even as they think they are being friendly, what they are saying is: *I allow you to be here, I allow it.* They say you are one of their family and they are angry if you ask for overtime pay.

Glory!

'Kovrin,' he says again. He gulps water from his mug. 'It was Kovrin.'

These days, in her emails, Yaryna often says to me, *Why don't you come to Austria, there is work here, you should come.* She is happy there, she says, her health is better, the air is clean. Maybe I will go. One day I will go home.

'Yes,' I say. 'It was him. I've told you everything now, that's all.'

At this time of day, when the evening comes, if I look through the window at the gasworks, the skeleton of it, the metal bars look to me like a spaceship, a chance to escape. Subject not object. I am ready.

5. The Virgin

1 December

SIMON PASSED through the gate in the bell tower of St. Sophia's, powder blue against the white sky, and crossed the silent courtyard. Several inches of snow lay on the ground, pristine but for the shallow imprint of birds' feet. He entered the cathedral and stomped his boots on the mat, disoriented, momentarily, by the sepulchral interior, the frescoes blurring in the vaulted shadows, the whiff of incense that nauseated before it tranquilised. The gloom was offset by the gilt of the iconostasis, its golden sheen illuminating the murk.

He peered into the side chapels. Kovrin wasn't there. Two elderly women in headscarves lit candles in the chancel, mumbling incomprehensible prayers.

'Thank you so much for coming.'

Thibaut was standing behind him, close to a scale model of Kiev in the time of ancient Rus. Simon removed his hat.

'Don't mention it. But this is rather a busy afternoon, as I'm sure you can appreciate, with all the ministers in town. I'm afraid I—'

'Mr Kovrin will be here in a moment,' Thibaut said. 'Only a moment. He prefers to talk upstairs. If you don't mind.'

He indicated the aisle that ran behind the pillars at the rear of the cathedral. Simon complied, passing beneath the blank gaze of fading archangels, his footsteps clattering on the iron tiles with their mysterious, zodiacal designs. He found the spiral stairwell and climbed up to the balcony. Thibaut followed.

'Cold today, no?' Thibaut said. 'Colder than yesterday, I think.' He smiled.

'Quite possibly,' Simon said. 'He's on his way, you say?' He drew back his coat sleeve to look at his watch.

Below them, the machine-gun rap of Kovrin's heels on the tiles heralded his approach. He emerged from the staircase, trailing two bodyguards, steepling his hands in pantomime supplication as he crossed the balcony towards them.

'Simon! My friend!'

He spread his arms as if for an embrace. Simon decommissioned his hands into his pockets.

'Thibaut,' Kovrin said, 'could you ...'

He flicked his head towards a man in dungarees and wire-rimmed spectacles, perched on a stepladder to restore a panel of the balcony's ceiling. Engrossed, the man seemed not to have noticed their entrance. Thibaut strode over and called up to him; the man glanced at Kovrin, pressed his glasses to the bridge of his nose and scuttled down the ladder and away, leaving his paints and brushes behind. Thibaut hovered at the top of the staircase, gloves dangling from his hand. He undid his coat. The bodyguards retreated into the shadows by the wall, their faces blending with the pallid frescoed saints.

'She's beautiful, no?' Kovrin leaned on the stone parapet that overlooked the mosaic in the apse. The Virgin's halo and shawl were shaped in gold against a golden background. 'She's one thousand years old. One thousand! From my point of view, she's very beautiful.'

Simon met the heavy-lidded, Asiatic eyes in the Virgin's mannish face. The harmlessly narcotic aroma of incense wafted from the chapels. Kovrin crossed himself.

'Magnificent,' Simon said. 'Now what was it you wanted—'

'Is because of love, you know that? Why Vladimir, famous prince, why he took us into our church. Love for one woman, he wanted to marry her. Anyway, it's what they say.' He looked aslant at Simon. 'People will do all things for love. Men. We.'

Simon grunted in lieu of agreement.

'You know,' Kovrin continued, resting on his elbows and twiddling his thumbs, 'I tried to buy her one time. Bishop said in principle yes, but we couldn't agree her price. I wanted her for my bathroom.'

Kovrin waited a few seconds before slapping a hand on the parapet. 'Is joke!' He patted Simon's back. 'I fool you! She is priceless, thousand years old. Nobody can buy ... So far.'

Simon turned back to the Virgin in her glistening blue robe, her hands aloft, her unexpected red shoes. 'What is it we can do for you, Mr Kovrin? This time. I'm listening.'

'Absolutely,' Kovrin said. 'Business first. So, I must tell you, once again is new context. Today is very dramatic, very effi-cient. This is a fact.'

That morning, the poisoned candidate and the woman with the braid had led a march up the hill from the square to parlia-ment. The crowd had overflowed the tarmac, scuffling along the grass verge and through the denuded park above the road.

The riot police stood firm outside the monumental government headquarters, halfway up Hrushevsky Street, but out of awe or sympathy the guards at the parliament building let the leaders through. Inside the chamber the candidate swore a symbolic oath of office, a scrum of his supporters defending the podium from punch-throwing allies of the bandit. Other protesters seethed around the Supreme Court, inside which the judges were still deliberating.

'New context means another new concept. So.' He held his hands open, palms up, a gesture that combined surrender with munificence. 'He will be prime minister, your man. Prime minister.'

'He is not our man, as I believe I've explained to you before.'

'Wait, please, is more. Prime minister now and, in two years, new elections. Then, nobody knows. Maybe president. Probably.'

'They want him to be president now.'

'Also now will be new rules of the game. New constitution – more power for prime minister, that means for him. President will be like your queen of England, waving, signing laws. Show time – tourists. Okay, not so many tourists. Afterwards, if your friend is president, he can go to old rules, take all his power back.'

Not merely a tweak to the results. Not a rerun with alternative candidates. A panicky, Hail Mary reform of the constitution. Capitulation, almost but not quite complete.

'To be clear, your – the government's candidate would be content with this arrangement?'

'Absolutely he is content. Absolutely content.'

The tipping point had arrived; the point at which split-second decisions might determine a person's fate, or the fate of a nation. Stick or twist, defect or don't, follow or disobey orders – it was a decision either way. Functionaries from the old administration were materialising on the stage in Independence Square, linking arms, singing the national anthem, devoid of shame. A turncoat minister wept, begged pardon, and dried his eyes with an orange scarf. Each side was threatening the other with prosecution: 'Only God forgives,' Vlasych growled when the BBC asked about an amnesty for the *ancien régime*. Meanwhile, violence had infiltrated the capital. A dozen people were in hospital, four of them in comas, after *titushky* clubbed an orange picket outside the electoral commission.

'Leave it with me. I understand the urgency, we can see the situation is critical. We'll put your idea into the mix.'

'The mix ...' Kovrin drummed his fingers on the parapet. 'Off records?' he stage-whispered. 'To tell the truth, I like your guy. Frankly speaking, I like him more. Civilised person, normal person. With such people it is possible to do business. But, I must tell you, this is our chance for compromise. Last chance, maybe.'

'There's no such thing as a last chance, in my view. But as soon as I get a response I will let you have it. You have my word.'

An attendant in a blue shawl, matching the blue of the Virgin's, crossed the balcony and approached them. Thibaut sprang from the stairs to intercept her. She glided away in silence.

'Is okay,' Kovrin said. 'I make contribution, regular contribution.' He mimed writing a cheque. 'You know, princes used to stand up here, they pray in secret. Like us.'

'Fascinating, really, though I'm not a prince, Mr Kovrin, nor was meant to be. Only a humble diplomat. But one question, if I may, on your plan. Two years – why two years? The rationale.'

'Two years is enough. To find buyers at fair price, market price. Otherwise, your orange friends, they take everything for nothing – the factories, mines. Aluminium. Telephone spectrum. For myself, I am protected, nothing of mine is from privatisations, that is what they will punish. All from secondary markets. But others in power worry, believe me.'

'No Western government – not us, not the Americans – will endorse the expropriation of private property. Whoever becomes president, you can rest assured about that.'

Beneath them, on the cathedral floor, a bearded priest emerged from a chapel and bustled across the tiles towards the sarcophagus of Yaroslav the Wise.

'Endorse, not endorse … Simon, Mr Davey, please, you understand, in this country, in countries like mine, is not one kind of money, is two. There is money in streets, in pockets, money to buy *horilka*, *salo*, money to buy *kvass*. Money in pensions – okay, maybe not so much in pensions.' He tutted. 'This is ordinary money, you understand this. Inflation, economy, so on. Then there is second type, big money, money in factories, money in offshore bank, in Cyprus. You cannot forget this money. In the ends, this money will decide.'

'I understand the interests at stake here, I do. That is why, in our view – and I know you disagree – but in our view, the court, as a neutral institution—'

'You understand? Good. Means you know, big money is not only money. Means lives. For this type of person, is not competition. The square, this election. Is not some game. For this type of person, this is war. Absolutely war. You think they worry to go to prison? No. They worry to die. To be killed. Not by your friends – they worry to be killed by *their* friends. Each knows what his friends have stolen, when, how. Each worries that, to save himself, his friend may talk. If revolution happens, to stop all talking, some of them may die.' He raised his chin and drew a finger across his throat. 'Give them two years, they will find better ways – they sell, they move abroad – it can be that nobody dies.'

'Yes, I see now. Transition planning, you might call it.'

'Nobody dies later – and nobody dies now. It means, on the square. Because there they can also die, you know that? Without compromise, they can die, as I warned already. Soon, maybe very soon. Not this few in hospital – many in the ground. Who knows?' He looked the Virgin in the eye.

'That would be a tragedy,' Simon said. 'For everyone.'

'Absolutely. But some people – powerful people – they want to end this story that way. They prefer it – to make a show in blood. And better to be your blood than theirs.'

Simon gripped the parapet. 'The consequences would be grave, as I'm sure you realise. Including for business. But, as I say, I will pass on your thoughts.'

'Quickly, please. Do it quickly.' Kovrin shoved his hands into the pockets of his coat. 'Because I like them, your people. Nice people. Remind me her name, that little one? Your little friend.'

Simon flushed. 'She is not my friend, I think you might have misconstrued things. We met her through our outreach scheme.'

'Technical question,' Kovrin said.

He descended the stairs, positioned between the two bodyguards in such a way that, from Simon's perspective above him, he seemed to have vanished, as in an optical illusion.

Together they walked back across the courtyard. The sky had darkened to slate while they were in the cathedral. The percussion of the street, the sirens and exhortatory car horns, scarcely penetrated the compound.

They passed through the bell tower. Kovrin's SUV had pulled across the kerb and onto the forecourt. The men convened around its open back door.

'This is good offer, I think. Best offer.'

'Clearly a lot of thought has gone into it.'

'Is good offer for you also. For you, for your family.'

Simon paused. Kovrin climbed into the back seat. 'I'm not altogether sure what you mean by that.'

Kovrin let the threat hang in the air before he finessed it. 'I mean only, is final offer, Mr Davey. You want to help, shiny armour? Help this plan. Call us. Tell us. Call Thibaut.'

'A pleasure,' Thibaut said, his teeth shining ghoulishly under the street lights. 'As always.' He joined his boss in the car.

The embassy was in an impractical old mansion, the offices carved out higgledy-piggledy from the former reception rooms. The diplomats shared them, for the most part, groups of two or three crammed together in cubbyholes. But Iain had his own office. He needed it.

'On my desk,' Jacqui said. 'I found your note. About the security breach.'

'Close the door,' Iain said.

'That bad, is it?' Her forced chuckle came out as a cough. She shut the door and leaned against it.

'Sit down ... There, good lass.'

She crossed her legs. 'I think there's been some sort of—'

'Hold your horses,' Iain said, raising a hand. 'Just a fireside chat, nothing formal, just to clear things up. You know we have to take precautions, even more with all this drama going on – I know you know, but just let me, will you? My job.' She nodded. 'Okay. We've got to assume they've all been compromised – I mean, our local staff. By the home team you know, or the Russians. Both, could be. Or will be, once the heavies start asking about the welfare of their kiddies or their wee cat or threaten to evict their grandmother. Pets especially. Pets are a favourite.'

'I know.'

'The driver, Lida the cook – those rosy cheeks, you know, the Friar Tuck haircut, always telling you off for not eating enough – they've been here for ever, they know everything, both of them, and everything they know ...'

'I didn't—'

'... it's all in a file somewhere. Every snog under the mistletoe at the Christmas party. All of it. Which means you never—'

'That's what I'm—'

'Just let me, okay? Over and done with. They can hear us, did you know that? They could hear us now if they wanted to. Not just the talking either, they can pick up the taps of your keyboard and put them back together again. One of their big microphones, electromagnetic thingamies. Everywhere except in the box and the comms room. So, one, you never take anyone in there, goes without saying.' He raised a thick finger for each security rule he enumerated. 'You never leave restricted documents on your desk.' Two fingers formed a fuck-off V; after a moment Iain spun them round into a Churchillian victory sign. 'You always log out. Always. And you have to – just listen, Jacqui – you never leave the secure cupboard open. Never.' Two more fingers.

'I didn't.'

'Someone saw it. You were out of the room and it was open.'

'Who? Who saw it?'

He smiled but said nothing.

'Was it Simon? I bet it was Simon.'

Iain sat back in his chair. 'Don't fly off the handle now.'

'He's got it in for me, no matter what I do – you must be able to see that, surely?'

'Jacqui,' he said, 'have a care.'

She rolled her wedding ring between the thumb and fore-finger of her other hand. 'In any case, it can only have been for a moment, I don't think this is fair.'

'Jacqui,' he repeated, leaning forward, 'everybody gets these. Breaches like this. They're like speeding tickets, you're in the fast lane, you're not thinking. When I was in Buenos Aires – I could tell you stories.' He shook his head fondly. 'The office doesn't get involved unless you really start racking them up.'

'The office knows?'

'It's just protocol.'

'Oh God, it's on my record?'

'Everyone gets them.'

She covered her glasses. 'Is this why I wasn't asked to the Vlasych meeting?'

'No, no, nothing like that. Not for the time being. Just a fireside chat.'

Simon strode across the plaza, past the statue of the Cossack hetman, pointing eternally towards Moscow from his saddle, past Olga, the half-mythic princess, stolid in her marble, and up the side of the foreign ministry. Ahead of him, Andriyivsky Descent zigzagged down to Podil, the embankment district that had been largely Jewish until the war. At the top of the slope, St Andrew's church strained towards the sky, like a turquoise-domed spaceship lifting off for a better world.

Voices were raised behind him as he approached the embassy, followed by a scream. Like the cry an infant makes after banging her head – the beginning swallowed in shock, so that half the sound seems lost – the scream was unfinished, cut off by a blow or a hand over the screamer's mouth. Simon turned and jogged back towards the ministry on the compacted snow. He reached the plaza in time to see two uniformed men hurling a limp-limbed civilian into the back of a van, his head thudding on the frame. One of the goons climbed in, a hand on his truncheon. The other slammed the doors from the outside and the van sped off; he caught sight of Simon, spat on the ground and walked away.

Simon hurried along Desyatynna Street, hailed the guard and went into the embassy. He told the ambassador about the incident in the plaza and relayed Kovrin's proposal, and his threats; he left a message for his American counterpart. Already, diplomats were pinballing across the city at high speed – hastily briefed foreign ministers, high representatives of the European Union, freelancing American senators exhilarated by the Cold War reprise. Emissaries of the Kremlin flew in like square-suited angels of death. They emerged from talks in the presidential administration to make identikit statements about the sanctity of the people's will. They wielded the people against each other like a mace.

Iain intercepted Simon in the corridor between the ambassador's office and Simon's own.

'Kovrin again, today? Bosom buddies, these days, the two of you.'

'On the contrary, I rather think we ought to have kept him out of the country. Pulled strings to get his visa, you know. His charities, the great and the good.'

'Conniving little bugger.'

'As I say, I don't disagree. But for the moment he's our back channel.'

'If you say so. But how are you then? Anyway.'

'Fine, thank you. Perfectly.'

'Head still sore?'

Simon forced out a laugh. 'Of course not. Not in the least.'

Iain cocked his chin, stroked his moustache and said nothing. His eyes were rheumy but penetrating.

'One-off,' Simon went on. 'Slightly blindsided by the liquor, that's all. Bit of exhaustion, probably. Won't happen again.'

'I know it won't.' Iain propped an elbow against the wall, a jowly cheek resting on his palm, a posture that, beneath its nonchalance, insisted the conversation was not over. 'So, who was the lass again?'

'Which lass?'

Iain arched an eyebrow.

'I already told you. Student activist – you remember, from the other night. Jacqui met her in Lviv. Useful insight into the mood.'

'She's Jacqui's contact, then?'

'In a manner of speaking.'

Simon had seen Olesya again the previous day, this time at his instigation, in a park overlooking the river, uphill from parliament and the court.

'I've made some inquiries,' he had told her. 'About your friend. Yaryna, wasn't it?'

'We thank you.' She shivered in her thin coat.

'There's a media fellowship in America, North Carolina. There would be a stipend, health insurance. We could recommend her.'

'This for Yaryna will be paradise. Music, American films, she loves them. Motown. Michael Jackson.'

'Let's wait and see.'

They were standing alongside a dry fountain, beneath a bulbous street lamp. Snow had settled on the sloping trunks of trees and the ledges of the balconies that overlooked the park; it lay like flying carpets on the roofs of idling police cars beyond the fence. A *babusia* pushed a pram around the fountain, humming to its occupant.

'Moreover,' Simon said, 'moreover, one wanted – I wanted – to apologise. For the other evening. To say sorry.'

'Sorry for what?'

'For any discomfort. In the bar, I got rather carried away. Not my intention.'

She touched his arm. 'It's nothing.'

After she left him he had ambled to the barrier above the river. Between the white-dusted trees and the pregnant sky, the grey water was the horizon's darkest feature. He had gripped the railing at the edge of the ravine and watched his breath crystallising in the air.

'Best leave her to Jacqui, maybe,' Iain said in the corridor at the embassy. He straightened up. 'Word to the wise.'

'Understood.'

Iain tapped Simon lightly, once, afterwards hovering his hand above his colleague's shoulder as if intending to bring it down again. He smiled and loped away.

'You always think that,' Jacqui was saying, 'but I'm not ... I said, I'm not ... No, when the foreign secretary comes over, watch, they won't let me in the room ... Martin, for the last time, I'm not imagining it. You should hear the way he speaks to me – do this, do that ... I know it's not your fault ... I told you about the girl, she was my contact, not his, now he's got me tracking down exchange programmes for some friend of hers. Meanwhile he's swanning ... For crying out loud, it's not in my head ... Yes, I wish you were here too – that's another thing, they expect you to drop everything, do some little vanity project ... Wait, someone's coming ... Wait.'

After a year or two in the embassy they all learned to discriminate among their colleagues' footsteps: the feline patters, dragging shuffles, or, in the ambassador's case, an officer-class clop, each with its unique algorithm of heel and personality.

'Right,' she whispered, 'I've got to ... I'll try, I will, but half the time it's like I'm invisible. This security thing is the last straw ... Yes, I'm sure it was him – Iain didn't deny it. As if he's such a saint ... I said it's the last ... I know you do ... You too ... Miss you too.'

She hung up and arrived at the door of her office as Simon passed it.

'Simon, there you are. Just checking, is there a line to take?' Her hair curled at her ears, but the hours it had spent beneath her beret flattened it across her crown. She smoothed her skirt.

'Excuse me?' On the wall behind him, a poster advertised student exchanges.

'The negotiations. Phone's off the hook. That tosser Thompson has called four times.'

'Look,' Dorian Thompson had said to her an hour earlier, 'if there's a breakthrough and you only give it to one other paper, we can call it an exclusive. Or two, okay two, if they're broadsheets.'

'Right,' Jacqui had said. 'Got it.'

'On the other hand, if you think they're going to kill each other, let me know so I can square away the picture desk.'

'I'm afraid not,' Simon told her. 'Nothing yet – 3D chess, you know. Lots of moving parts.'

He looked absently over her shoulder into her office.

'It's all ship-shape in there,' Jacqui said. 'I'm only human, you know.'

'What was that? Sorry.'

'Nothing.' She sighed. 'Actually, all this donkey work reminds me of the NATO summit in Prague. I was in the delegation but I got stuck in a hangar with the hacks.'

'Sorry to hear that.' He pinched his nose.

'I'm sure you are. Right then.'

No. No from the Americans; no from the opposition. No outcome other than a rerun of the election was acceptable, and now, not in two years' time. No new candidates. No. They would wait for the Supreme Court to rule.

Simon sat at his desk, a picture of Nancy propped up in front of him, dull lunar light ghosting through the high, solitary window in his office. He dialled the number he had for Kovrin.

Thibaut answered. 'Excellent to hear you,' he said. 'How are you?'

'I have a message for Mr Kovrin,' Simon said. 'Might I—'

'Yes, yes of course. A moment.'

Down the line a conversation in Russian was curtailed, someone told someone else to wait, a television was muted or turned off.

'I'm listening,' Kovrin said. 'Simon.'

He conveyed the response, in terms euphemistic enough to confound the phone-tappers but plain enough for Kovrin to understand.

'Bullshit.'

'We think it's in everyone's interests,' Simon said, 'to maintain order. No rash moves on any side. We hope you will use your influence.'

Silence. Breathing.

After thirty seconds Kovrin spoke. 'You understand this situation, I think. You are man of the world. Someone will be winners here, yes? From my point of view, when is winners, means also will be losers. Victims. It's war, as I told you. War.'

Simon put his feet up on the desk. He would not panic or beg. In the photo in front of him, Nancy was poised to throw a snowball, made of paper, in a school play. Six, maybe seven. When he had taken the picture, he had thought that he could never love her more.

'Mr Kovrin, I am only passing on what I've been told. I'm afraid the trust is gone. The poisoning – even if it was, er, outside agents – one can see how that would make them feel. But as I said in the cathedral, there's always another chance, and I hope we can keep this channel o—'

Kovrin clicked his tongue. 'It's clear,' he said, and hung up.

Back, warily, along the edge of the plaza, beneath the gaze of the mounted Cossack; past the peach ministerial building and the bar with the piano on the pavement. A man was sitting at the snow-speckled keyboard, alone, in a balaclava and fingerless gloves, picking out the 'Ode to Joy'. Simon lingered, his nose running, ears burning from the cold. The piano player did not look up.

Up the pock-marked stairs and into their apartment. He hung up his coat (years ago they had bought the hat stand at an auction house, feeling faintly rakish, afterwards shipping it around with them like a relic of that time). He went into the kitchen. Cynthia had laid the table: one plate, one knife, one fork.

'I wasn't expecting you.'

'Might be a late night – we're in the endgame now – thought I'd look in while I could.'

Cynthia rose from the table, cracked open the door of the oven and peeked inside. She rearranged the glove on the handle and sat down. Simon moved towards the telephone.

'You won't get her tonight. Outdoor orienteering thing – useful for university entrance, she said.'

'She'd better not climb any trees. *High as the sky* – do you remember, that's what she used to say? Scared the living daylights out of me.'

'That was a long time ago.' Her shoulders were hunched, as if against a chill, or a raptor.

'Well, let's hope this is all put to bed before Christmas. But if we can't get back, you could show her the churches. There'll be something at the embassy.'

'Yes,' Cynthia said. She swallowed; the knot in her scarf bobbed at her neck. 'She can meet your colleagues.' She picked up her fork, then laid it back down with a crack.

'Cynthia.'

'That was the worst thing,' she said. 'Of all the things. That you mixed her up in it.'

'We've been through this umpteen times,' Simon said. 'I did not mix her up, I did not intend to. She was just ... They were both there, that's all. They barely talked.'

'Talking wasn't the problem, was it? Of course, you said it was over, then. That's what you said.'

'It was over. It had been.' He stroked his beard. 'Look, it's been quite a trying day, this really isn't the moment ... I'm sorry, I shouldn't have said that ... Darling ... I ...'

'That's the trouble,' she said, looking down at her lap. 'If you think about it. How do I know?'

He stepped forward and put a hand on her shoulder. She raised her own hand and laid it on his, grasped it, then cast it off. She stood and took her dinner from the oven.

With her back to him she said, 'You can't get proper ricotta.'

'I'm sorry,' Simon said again. 'Anyway they're expecting me, I'd better ...'

He put on his coat and walked back to the embassy.

An hour later, a figure in an aviator hat emerged from a car outside the Philharmonic and paced towards Independence Square. The steel band in the park pumped out its cardiac beat. The volunteers at the Lenin Museum dispensed blankets and borscht. En route to the square he passed a group of women dancing in a circle, like some Arctic, bescarfed Matisse. The people on the road made way for him; he looked like a politician, or a spook, with his upright bearing and insincere smile. A person to avoid. He passed a protester in an orange Santa suit, a girl in an orange wig, a policeman with an orange ribbon tied to his epaulette.

The crowd was thick, and he was obliged to edge sideways, leading with his shoulder. On the stage the woman with the braid was apostrophising 'the people': these people, here and now, but also a mythic people, the people they wanted to become.

'We are not tired, we are not scared. We are strong. We have no choice.'

Glory!

'We will build our own future,' the woman exclaimed. Behind her on the stage, the chocolate tycoon raised his fists. 'We will not go back to their past!'

Shame!

The sonic boom of a nation escaping its history.

Thibaut stood on tiptoe to scan the banners sailing above the square. He located the one from Ivano-Frankivsk, held aloft in front of the Conservatory. To reach the spot, he skirted the steps around the monument; someone had scaled the column and draped an orange flag from the statue of the goddess. The politician with the braid made way for a priest.

Nearing the group with the banner he made out a young woman in purple earmuffs, but not the person he wanted. He approached a man in a leather coat who was holding one of the banner poles, an orange ribbon tied around his forehead, an orange band at his bicep.

'Excuse me,' Thibaut said. The crowd intoned an *Amen* in response to the priest's benediction. 'I'm looking for a young woman named Olesya. She told me she would be here this evening.'

He smiled. Their breaths mingled between them.

'Who is asking?'

'A friend.'

'What friend? I don't know this friend.'

Olesya came round from behind the banner and appeared next to Andriy. Her hat was off, her hair down, her face pinched from sleeplessness and the cold.

'Ah,' Thibaut said. 'Here she is.'

'In your text,' Olesya said to him, 'you tell me we must talk. About what?'

Yaryna shuffled over to stand at her other side. 'You've got a lot of fans,' she said to Olesya. 'I'm starting to get jealous. Who's this one?'

East and West are together!

Olesya had to shout above the chanting. 'What is this? What are you doing here?'

'A quick word,' Thibaut said. 'Very quick. But private, please.'

Yaryna linked her arm with Olesya's. 'Should I come with you?'

'Only you,' Thibaut insisted. 'No one else.'

'No,' Andriy said. 'Enough with these secret meetings.'

'It's very important,' Thibaut said. 'Urgent, I promise you.'

'I'm asking you, Lesechka,' Andriy pleaded. 'They're not our friends, these people.'

Olesya reached up and stroked her brother's hair. She squeezed Yaryna's hand.

'I'll be okay,' she said. 'I'm sure of it.'

Thibaut ushered her towards the colonnade on the Conservatory's facade.

v. The cage

IF, LIKE nations, individuals need their histories, they also, like nations, take comfort in their grudges. Grudges are a crutch against the arbitrariness of fate, its vertigo. Yet they are more than that, in my experience – not just a crutch but the scaffold of one's identity, less a prop than the person himself. In my solitary years, as my nobler feelings have atrophied, I have sensed my own personality contracting to a suite of grievances: against the office and its farcical hearing, against Cynthia for her obduracy, against Olesya for her betrayal. Against myself.

Evidently, however, I have leaned too heavily on Olesya. This is, so to speak, a structural blow. The scaffold is in danger of toppling over, if the plank is not replaced.

She sits cross-legged on her bed, regarding me as if I were a patient emerging from a coma, and she the compassionate relative at my bedside.

'You could have told me the truth from the beginning,' I say. 'I would have understood.' In my heart, though, I know the jig is up, so far as Olesya goes, poor girl. I thought she had betrayed me to bolster her cause, ingratiate herself with her comrades, both. But plainly she is as much his victim as I was – more. And it was me who introduced them, as she said.

'I told you what I had to, do you see? I had no choice.'

Someone, a man, thumps up the stairs and rattles the bathroom door. Another man responds from within. It is not a friendly exchange.

'Well,' I say, 'if I'm going to get to the bottom of this, I'll have to see Kovrin. Is he in London, do you know?'

She jolts upright. 'You can't.'

'So he's here?'

'As far as I know, yes, but ... I thought you understood. He will know it was me who told, and he is ... You know what he is, I don't have to say.'

'I know what he was. That was a long time ago.'

I recall, at the embassy, playing a mordant little game, a skit, concerning the so-called murder test. That is to say, we would speculate as to whether such-and-such a person – an oligarch, a politician, a crook, frequently all three at the same time – had ever committed, or commissioned, murder. Those deemed to have blood on their hands failed the test. Someone – perhaps it was that woman, the public affairs officer – proposed Kovrin, and the rest of us, older hands, guffawed. Kovrin! The notion that Kovrin might pass the murder test!

'A fox will always eat chickens. I'm asking you, Simon.' Her eyes appear bloodshot, though as yet there are no tears. Young women from her country, countries like hers, they are older than their counterparts here – they see more in the same spell on Earth, there is more that they are obliged to tolerate. 'Leave him,' she implores. 'Please.'

How long, in London, would be the phone-call chain between Kovrin's wrath and ultraviolence? In Kiev, in the olden days, I would have thought that there were zero links in that chain, no phone calls required, merely a grimace to his consigliere. Turbulent priest, and all that. In London ... three? The first call to his fixer, a second to an intermediary, a third to the muscle. Four maybe. Five at the outside.

'Please,' she repeats.

Now the tears seep out, try as she does to stifle them. The old paternal instinct is there to comfort her, I feel it.

'Listen,' I say. Briskly she wipes her eyes. 'I see your point of view, I do. But look at it from his perspective. Kovrin's. Why would he connect me with you? Now, I mean.'

Brave girl.

'You don't know what he knows,' she says. 'And if he does know, this is it. This is what I have.'

She waves a hand around the room, an ironically grand gesture for her borstal quarters. A solitary cloud has congealed in the early-evening sky, hovering beside the gasworks like a monster's speech bubble. Belatedly I notice a shape protruding from beneath Polly's pillow: a worn, beige, beanbag rabbit.

'Think about it, he must have been behind the whole thing – the leaks, all of it. I could have been tipped off by someone in Kiev, put two and two together. I won't breathe a word about you, on my honour.'

'On your honour ...' she drawls.

The room is not chilly, not at all, but she wraps her arms around herself as if she were shivering on the square. She closes her eyes. A train rumbles along the edge of the park, taking people home to their families.

She opens her eyes and stands. 'Okay. If you want to, go. Go if you have to. Maybe I won't be here so long anyway.'

'You're leaving?'

'Let's see. It's been more than three years here, maybe it's enough.'

'I doubt that he will even see me.'

'Who knows? He lives how he likes.'

Means war.

She moves to the bedroom door. A metallic crash emanates from the kitchen – I envisage a tower of washed-up pots collapsing. Someone laughs. Someone else curses.

'If you like,' she says at the door, 'if you want, I may write a letter. I mean, to your daughter. I may tell her there was nothing with us. I don't know if she will believe it. But if you like, I may.'

Momentarily I am nauseous with shame: considering how the afternoon began, this is unlooked-for kindness. I would like to think hers is a good idea. I would like to think it could make a difference. But for Nancy, I fear, the statute of limitations has expired. The case is closed.

'Thank you,' I stutter, stricken by her generosity. 'Very kind of you. May I think about it? Very kind indeed.'

She brushes past me to the bookcase, finds a notepad and rips out a small piece of paper, the kind of scrap one invariably loses. She scribbles and hands me a note. Her email address. I stand and put the paper in my pocket. 'Thank you.'

'Your bag,' she says. I pick it up.

I follow her onto the landing and we descend the creaky stairs. A vase of plastic flowers and a porcelain Virgin stand on the windowsill at the bottom, along with a small, gurning model of a dolphin, the sort of trinket one used to find in cornflake packets.

'Thank you for your time,' I say, and we both smile at my formality.

'It's nothing.' She opens the front door, letting in the summer air.

'Do you think – may I ask? – do you think it was worth it? What we did that night. Do you think this way, all this, the war, is better than what might have happened otherwise?'

After the killing that spared Andriy, after that bandit had run away, the Russians invaded. In Kiev, the people pulled down the Lenin statue, beneath which I once waited for Kovrin, they smashed it to smithereens – and in short order they got a war. Now, I gather, the square is an outdoor memorial to the shooting, a holy place, rimmed with shrines to the martyrs. They turned the bandit's palace into a museum of corruption. I remember the man who drove us to the airport all those years ago, Cynthia and I on the back seat, pressed against opposite doors, telling us that it couldn't last – his country, that is – that it would surely fall apart, and I felt confident, as the forest blurred past, that he was wrong.

She does not hesitate. 'It's not a real question.' *Technical question.* 'We couldn't know what would follow. And it must be better to try, no? In the end, it's better to try.'

'Perhaps,' I say, though I am not so sure.

We stand at the open door. She moves first – a hand on my shoulder, then both of them, reaching around my back as she enfolds me. Despite what the world inferred, I have held her as I do now only once before, on that same night, at the embassy. It was my closest encounter with another body for months, Nancy being away at school, Cynthia marooned on the far side of our cryogenic bed, the primal need for human touch long left unrequited. We embraced, and Olesya skipped back to her brother and the square.

'Thank you,' I whisper.

That citrus scent again, which I detected on the platform this afternoon, one of those elastic afternoons that seem to last a decade. She has a closed-up piercing in her ear. I register the pulse in her white neck. I sense, and try to unsense, her front pressed firmly against mine.

It's all a matter of smell.

Involuntarily I envisage her and Kovrin, there in the apartment on Baseina Street, the little gifts he must have brought her (lingerie, one supposes). Whatever went through her mind as she watched the shadows dance on the ceiling. I am loath to think about it.

She pulls away and I look into her eyes, pouched in their dark rings. 'Good luck,' I say. 'Whatever you do next. You deserve it, really.'

'Thank you,' she says. 'And with your daughter.'

We have an inkling, cradling our children, that our lives now repose in their clenched, dollish hands. But only later do we understand. *You're the best daddy in the world!*

'I'm sorry.'

'You are always sorry. The English.'

Again she grasps my shoulder but now her body maintains its distance.

'I'm sorry,' I repeat, gathering up my swimming bag.

She is still in the doorway when I look back from the pavement. She raises a hand but does not wave, diverting it instead to tuck stray hair behind her ear. It occurs to me that she might be making sure that I have left. Ten paces on, as I reach a car covered by a tarpaulin, I turn again and she is closing the door. I can see her arm, her hand and wrist, finally her fingers on the doorframe, and she is gone.

I ghost past the teenagers occupying the benches in the park. In the shopping precinct, outside the church that supervises the pawnbroker's, piercing studios and phone-unlockers, the flushed men we passed earlier are still congregating. The largest man has his head in his hands. Other people keep their distance – less out of fear, I suspect, than from a limbic instinct to separate themselves from misfortune.

I know that syndrome well: the telephone ceasing to ring, the friends who evanesce, Christmas cards that no long arrive, one's emails summarily ignored. As well as, conversely, the rare act of charity from an unexpected source.

Iain called me – Iain the security officer – this must have been April of the following year.

How are you over there?

Fine. Absolutely fine.

April or May, and at first I thought there must be more to come – a summons, possibly the police. A run-in with the Official Secrets Act. It would be up to others, they had indicated at the disciplinary hearing, to determine whether the public interest would be served by prosecuting me for my conduct. So far as I knew, no determination had been made. The police, I thought when I recognised his brogue, and after the police, prison.

Iain must have heard the apprehension in my voice, echoing down the line to Kiev, because he gave a little hooting chuckle.

No, I just wanted to see how you were keeping. No bother.

As well as can be expected. In the circumstances.

And since my drinking had yet to begin in earnest, and I was more or less compos mentis, I might even have been convincing.

Good lad. Be a good lad.

They were worried that I would kill myself, I imagine, an exit strategy that I had indeed considered. He was the only person from the office who called, and that was the only time. Twenty-four years, then poof! Erased like a purged commissar from a photograph.

Head still sore?

At those confidential meetings with Kovrin, which I diligently minuted and relayed, I had thought he would be the making of me. Now I see that, on the contrary, with one deft shove he dispatched me into the abyss.

Be careful. I should like to tell Nancy that – tell my daughter. *This life is a tightrope walk, so be very careful.*

I fish some change from my pocket, leave it on the church wall and press onwards to the station. I wait three minutes and board a train into town.

A good man in a crisis. I garnered my reputation in Washington and burnished it in Tel Aviv. There was a mini-summit at the embassy, and they sent out a novice minister from London – badly briefed, forgetful or both. In his opening remarks he strayed dangerously off script regarding the sovereignty of Jerusalem. I rose, whizzed around the table and murmured a correction in his ear. Afterwards he thanked me and wrote down my name.

I was buoyant. It was a warm, blue evening, not entirely unlike the one framed, today, by the window of my train carriage before it dips into the tunnel. A group of us went to a seafood restaurant in the old port, straight from the embassy, no spouses. One by one our colleagues left, the counsellors and secretaries making their excuses as they stumbled away, until there were only three of us on the terrace overlooking the water: the sort of impromptu festivity that is sweeter for its spontaneity and which, in one's gratitude for it, one wants desperately to prolong.

Well, goodnight, you two. Don't do anything I wouldn't do.

She laughed, which was I think the beginning of it. That banal, mindless remark.

Finish the bottle?

After that, we set off on the boardwalk, a stroll which, through the cabernet haze, I believe was my idea, though the kiss was not. Certainly not. Though nor did I resist. I was too astonished to resist: amazed that she would want me, and that I would find myself willing. Soon we were down on the shingle below the promenade, like teenagers.

Coast clear?

It's dark, Simon. Come on.

Thereafter a few clinches in the office, lunchtimes twice (I think) in her apartment, once, to my shame, in ours, photographs of Nancy reprimanding me from the mantelpiece. Then the confession to Cynthia and – worst of all – the hideous relapse. This liaison was a different proposition for the office, of course, because she was one of us. The person in question. She worked in the economic section of the embassy, which meant she had a security clearance too. Consenting adults, et cetera.

I can no longer see her face but I can smell her, if I close my eyes: sweat and salt and wine. And I can picture us, both of us, in the alcove where we kept the photocopier, her skirt rumpled up her back.

Go on then, quickly.

As I head, indignant, to my showdown with Kovrin – an encounter, I am well aware, that only one of us is expecting, and which therefore may never occur – I must acknowledge that he is not the only man to blame for my predicament. That rush of blood in Tel Aviv is the single event I would choose to undo if magically I were permitted to, the joker I would play in a do-over of my life.

The train arrives at Kovrin's station. I scurry up the steps from the platform, my bag swinging in my hand, then out into the city. Down I go to the river, gliding sludgily in the dimming light. The path on this side of the water is busy, but the world on the far bank is now an indistinct mesh of foliage. *Rus in urbe.*

The Thames, the Dnipro, the Potomac: the rivers that flow through cities all tend to have the same atmosphere, I find. The sense of history standing still, of essential things remaining the same, and, simultaneously, the feeling of time flowing away with the water, of secrets and suffering swept out to sea. At the beginning, for instance, I collected shards of detail about my father's life, knowing that if I didn't preserve them in my memory, nobody would. His life would be lost, as most lives are: it would disappear like a pebble thrown into the Thames. But before long I realised that these arcana were bound to die with me in any case, and I let the anecdotes and aphorisms wash away, such that I am left remembering only that something important has been forgotten.

Jacqui. Her name was Jacqui. The public affairs person. Her name *is* Jacqui, I assume. Something about a PhD.

Geese huddle beneath the river wall. The lights are on in the houseboats moored below the park. Only when I am through the alleyway and standing in front of Kovrin's house again – arrogantly square, like a town hall in a French village – do I realise that I have no plan of attack.

I consider vaulting the wall and rapping the brass knocker – shaped, I notice, like a gargoyle fish – but I reject this frontal strategy. They will not let me in. Quite possibly I will not reach the door before I am intercepted.

Instead I stand beneath the same antique street light on the river side of the road, beside the private garden that juts out onto the water, loitering like an extra in an impressionist street scene. When I last saw Kovrin, he and his fortune, indeed his whole country, were balanced like a ping-pong ball atop a jet of water. I recall him telling me that if there was going to be a winner on the square, someone would have to lose. I didn't realise, then, that one of the losers would be me. Evidently Kovrin himself was not among them.

I will wait for my chance.

The wait is not a long one. The sports car arrives, breaking only at the last moment, in a hurry as always, time is money. Time is life. Kovrin is driving, rather to my surprise, and (my luck is in) he screeches to a halt and parks outside rather than disappearing through the garage entrance in the wall. Straight away he is out, leaving the car door open for someone else to close, making for the front garden with his clockwork gait, which reminds me of those power-walkers one sees, every four years, in highlights of the Olympics. A rectangular body-guard in a tight suit levers himself out of the passenger seat. The garden gate is opened remotely as Kovrin approaches.

'Mr Kovrin?' I begin to run across the road from the street light – the thought is in my head that I must reach the gate before it closes – and this is my mistake. The running. The guard interposes himself. Through the ironwork of the gate I see another man emerge from a basement side-door and bound up the steps to the garden, like a troll whose trap is sprung.

They know their business, Kovrin's goons, one has to acknowledge that. The first man bends an arm behind my back and shoves me against the railings. 'Take it, take it,' I hear him say to his colleague in Russian, meanwhile twisting my arm higher up my back so that, certain it is about to snap, I scream. Out comes a high-pitched sound that I do not recognise as my own, the complaint of a wounded animal. It is the bag, I realise, the wretched swimming bag. I drop it and, momentarily, they stand apart, apparently fearing that it might explode. The second man, the troll, nudges the bag with his toe, then bends to look inside.

'*Bomzh*,' he says. A homeless man.

'Is not *bomzh*,' Kovrin says. He is standing on the other side of the gate, unruffled, an emperor watching his champions smite the chaff in the arena. 'I know this man. Absolutely.'

'Mr Kovrin,' I say, pleading my case as I was obliged to earlier, in the Polish deli. 'Might we talk?'

The arm-twister is peering up and down the street: scanning for witnesses, I assume, to whatever he anticipates doing to me next. I hear laughter from the alleyway, but no one else is abroad on this stretch of the river, and it is much too wide for anyone on the far bank to discern what is happening here.

'Talk? About what, "talk"?'

'About the square,' I say. 'About what happened that winter. A personal capacity, only.'

He looks me up and down, running a thumb over the knuckles of his hand.

'Please, Mr Kovrin. Five minutes. Misha.'

He smiles and checks his watch, tapping his foot on the pavement as he considers. Little upside, he must be figuring, but also zero risk.

'Okay,' he says. 'Five minutes. Forwards!'

The arm-twister, the shotgun-rider, resumes his grip and hustles me beneath the climbing roses that crown the gate, into the front garden and down the stairs that the troll ascended. I can feel his breath in my ear. I can feel the sweat seeping through his shirt and penetrating mine to mingle with my own – the warped, sub-erotic intimacy of the torturer and his victim. I do not cry out again. This, after all, is what I came for.

We scuffle through the side door into the security room. A suite of TV screens are arrayed on a wall, on one of which I catch sight of Kovrin mounting the front steps. He reappears, immediately, on another screen that captures the hallway. An empty pizza box and a cairn of Styrofoam cups, one of them torn into a coil by the troll's bored hand, lie on the table in front of the screens. They frisk me, roughly, extracting the wallet, keys and phone from my trousers and casting them onto the table. His palm spread across the base of my skull, the troll pushes me into a man-sized cage, or pen, which is fitted to the back of their office. Heart-stoppingly I register that Olesya's note, with her incriminating email address, has been missed in the sweep but dislodged, such that the scrap now protrudes from my pocket.

I won't breathe a word, I told her. *On my honour.*

As discreetly as I am able to, I tuck it back. They lock me in.

'Password?'

143

I tell them: Nancy's birthday. I notice a yellowed cigarette butt on the floor of the cage.

The troll turns off my phone.

For myself, I am not afraid. The cage reminds me of the type I occasionally glimpsed on the Metro in Kiev, inside the subterranean police posts in the stations, in which the constables restrained drunks or pickpockets or whichever unfortunates they had decided to shake down. The arm-twister wipes his brow with a paper tissue, buttons his jacket and leaves. I do not attempt to reason with the troll. I do not cry out. Plainly my wishes are of no particular account. I cradle my bent arm in the unmolested one – it is painful but not broken, so far as I can tell. I worry only that Kovrin will renege and decline to speak to me.

Odd, therefore, that I become alarmed when, after a quarter of an hour, I am brought upstairs. First we are in the hallway, familiar from the CCTV screens. It is entirely white, save for a large, silver-edged mirror and the ebony figurine I glimpsed this afternoon. An abstract circular sculpture, like a large breath mint, also white, rests on a white pedestal. The floorboards are stained white. The room has the ethereal air of the afterlife, as imagined in a psychedelic film. I am prodded into a study containing a huge Art Deco desk, a wall-mounted television and a bookcase too well ordered to be more than ornamental, like bookshelves in a country pub. In the corner stands a tripod-mounted globe. A rug decorated with a geometric pattern, reminiscent of Kandinsky, straddles the space between a coffee table and the fireplace. Perhaps it is a Kandinsky.

The troll nudges me through the study doors and – this is what disconcerts me most – closes them behind me, leaving me alone in the room. What I see here is evidently of no consequence. I am not entirely alone, of course: scanning the walls, I spot a CCTV camera mounted in the corner. I sit in one of the armchairs. The room puts me in mind, somehow, of Vlasych, her place in the mountains, with a lake, she said, and her boat. The whole country was a charnel house, she told us, yet there was hope. That was before her midnight flit, with her chiselled share of the loot, back to feather her nest in Westchester, New York.

Footsteps approach, light but sharp. A door opens and a forehead appears, then a high-heeled shoe. Natalia Kovrina offers me an automatic smile. She opens her mouth to address me but closes it upon realising (I presume) that she does not know my name, nor what I am doing in her home.

'Good evening, Mr ...'

'Hello.'

'We've met, I think.' She has shed her accent almost entirely. 'Have we?'

'We have.'

Her fingers caress the door handle. Her manner is that of an employee rather than a resident. Senior, but on duty. How harmless they must consider me.

'My husband ... is he in? I was not quite sure.'

'I believe so, yes.'

'Where was it, Mr ... Where was it that we met?'

'At your house,' I say. 'Outside Kiev. Some time ago now.'

'Of course.' She smiles again, briefly. 'If you will just ... So pleased ... Excuse me.'

She closes the door. The absence of footsteps tells me that she has stationed herself in the hallway. Possibly she is texting him, though Kovrin might not go in for text messages, security-wise. I recall him leaving his phone in the house when we walked together in the snow, tracked by his heavies, that rudimentary intimidation technique. Soon other footsteps approach, a fusillade that is surprisingly familiar after all of these years. Rat-a-tat-tat.

A rushed, hushed exchange in Russian that I do not quite follow. I make out only *You promised ... Supposed to be in Paris ... You said one week a month* (her), then *Urgent business ... Absolutely separate* (him). Then a sullen *Okay* (her), and the door reopens.

Kovrin paces to his desk and sits behind it as if I am not here. He does something on his computer, hurriedly, digits punching the keyboard in a rapid-fire spurt. He is somewhat greyer, creased around the eyes, but still lean and coiled. Between the slats of the blind I can see the black river, the yellow lights of the boats gliding up and down, yellow and orange, serene.

Turning from the computer, Kovrin indicates the chair facing his across the desk, lower and humbler than his high-backed throne. I move to sit in it. He closes his eyes, opening them as he recovers my name.

'So,' he says, 'Mr Davey. Tell me, please, how you find me here. This house.'

'Technical question,' I say. Kovrin smiles.

6. The box

1 December

OLESYA LEANED against the Conservatory's facade, her face framed by an advertisement for a piano recital, an artefact from a distant, civilian age. Thibaut positioned himself between her and the crowd. Behind him, groups of protesters shortcutted through the colonnade before burrowing into the square.

'Listen,' he said. 'It's necessary to be quick. It's tonight.'

Shame!

'What? I don't understand.'

'I said, it's tonight. The attack is tonight.'

'I can't hear you. What?'

Bandits out!

'They come tonight.' He glanced over each shoulder before raising his voice. 'They will attack the square. This.' With his eyes he indicated the sea of defenceless people. 'The government sends the soldiers this evening. Now.'

Glory!

She heard him. The noise of the square receded as she tuned into the warning, as when the bass line is turned down on a record.

'How do you know?'

'Mr Kovrin ... We know. For them it is the only way now – the government – they lost their other chances. They cannot make a deal. That's all.'

'Is it certain? There were too many rumours here.' She looked past him, towards the big screen, the banners, her friends. Her brother. Thibaut stepped closer to monopolise her view. The smell of burning from the braziers on Khreshchatyk seemed, at that moment, a harbinger of the inferno.

'They are already moving. Troops from the interior ministry. The order is given, they have left the barracks. Two, three hours and they will arrive. Maybe not so much. Listen to me. They will cross the river and come. Water cannon. APCs.'

Glory!

'Guns?'

'Of course, guns. Yes.'

He wiped his nose with the back of his glove. Olesya stared down at the paving stones in the colonnade, streaked in sanguineous slush.

'Andriy,' she said.

'Tonight.'

Together we are many!

Her chest heaved; she closed her eyes as if in prayer. They opened and looked up at him.

'Why are you ... What do you want with me?'

'Because we – Mr Kovrin – we think you can help. Look at me. Yes, you.'

She listened, inclining towards him as if for a kiss, as he explained where she was to go and what she must say. When he had finished, and repeated himself, enumerating the necessary steps with scything wags of his finger, he moved aside to let her pass. She surveyed the children hoisted on their parents' shoulders, earmuffed and woolly-hatted; at the rear of the crowd, a group of teenage girls were dancing a cramped conga.

'Okay,' she said. 'It's clear.'

Thibaut smiled. 'You go,' he said. 'You must go. You speak only to him, remember, no one else. But – only – one more thing, finally, please confirm it. You must not say we gave you this information. You must never say, not tonight, not ever. Never tell anyone, not him, not anyone. Mr Kovrin will be most upset. You understand? Angry.'

His fingers were locked in front of him as if to crack his knuckles. She swallowed. 'Okay,' she repeated. 'I will never.'

She was on her way, her scarf flung behind her dark coat, when the flaw presented itself.

'But,' she said, turning around, 'how will I say … How would I know …'

Thibaut clamped a hand on her forearm and pulled her back towards him, not gently. 'Yes, good. You say that it was the policeman. The riot policeman.'

'What? What policeman?'

'At the presidential administration. You gave him a rose, the young man, we saw you on television. The young man opposite you in the line. You talked. You talked, yes?'

'Only very little.'

'You told him where you are from.'

'I didn't tell—'

'You told him. It means he could find you in the crowd, same as I did, he knew you are from Ivano-Frankivsk. He liked you. He took off his uniform, he found you.'

'Yes, but how will he know about—'

'He has a cousin in the interior ministry troops, at the base where they are coming from. He spoke to this cousin, he remembered you, he felt sad, he came here.'

'Okay, his cousin.'

'It's enough, they can confirm it, use the satellites. They will tell the Americans.'

'And if he won't see me? Who then will help us – all these people – who will—'

'Don't think about that. Just go. Later we'll call you.'

She pivoted to leave but he tightened his grip. There was no pain, but when she tugged her arm she could not free herself. He held her gaze. 'Never. It is better for you – for you, understand? It's clear?'

'Clear.'

'Straight to the embassy,' he said as he released her. 'Stay away from your friends now. I'm watching you.'

Olesya left him in the colonnade and began to circumnavigate the square, heading for the road that led up to the embassy, but there were so many people, too many people, there was no way through them. They were Olesya's comrades, these people, her friends, but they were also her enemies, obstacles to their own salvation, too busy dancing, chanting, sculpting their ice statues, waving their banners, blithely banging their drums, to see that they were doomed. If you panned out from the scene you would see that this was a carnival held in a dragon's maw. She had to find a way around them, or soon they would not be a single, inviolable organism but a spray of human atoms – panicking IT developers, careening students, accountants stumbling over the curbs, no longer enacting their best selves but reduced to the most ragged. They would stampede for the entrance to the shopping centre at the back of the square, plunge into the Metro, huddle with the beggars in the underpasses, flood through the arches between the mansion blocks on Khreshchatyk. That is, if the archways had not already been barred by armoured trucks and men with truncheons. Perhaps they would block all the escape routes before the clubbing started. The arrests. The bullets.

The spell was about to break. As she pressed towards the stage she glanced up at the big screen. It showed another wide-angle shot of the square, tens of thousands of people swirling orange scarfs, holding aloft their flags and candles, grinning idiotically. Those burnished images were a movie, a fantasy of people-power, not the real, mortal thing.

We will not be defeated!

But they could be.

The church is near, but the way is icy.

The church is near, but the way is icy.

Olesya's grandmother was fond of that proverb, and it suited her mood as she began the ascent of Mykhailivska Street. She set off on the road but scuttled across the gutter and onto the pavement when a car approached. Some of the snow had melted, then frozen into an insidious black sheen, and, halfway up, she slipped. She had been leaning into the climb and fell forward as she lost her footing, bracing herself with her hands. She lay on the ground, stationary but with the momentary sensation of sliding backwards and away, back towards the square, the imminent interior ministry troops, possibly more than imminent, perhaps already in their positions. It began to rain – a sleety, lazy drizzle. It was as if she had made a misstep in a nightmarish game, tumbled down a ladder and into the snakes' lair. She picked herself up and returned to the road where the surface was truer. The lights of the Irish pub glinted ahead of her.

The church is near, but the way is icy.

She hesitated when she reached the perimeter of St. Michael's monastery, across the plaza from the foreign ministry. They looked like ordinary men, the riot police gathered beneath the ministry's Stalinist columns. One was laughing at a joke, another talking on his phone. She peered around the plaza, beyond the marble princess and towards the Cossack on horseback. These few men seemed to be the entire deployment. Probably they were not involved in the assault – were instead a mundane, blameless unit. Or maybe they would join in when the skull-cracking began, barrelling into the square from above, these ordinary blameless men, currently cooing goodnights to their children beneath the street lights. They were a bad omen. She fixed her eyes on the treacherous pavement and hurried into Desyatynna Street.

She had removed a mitten and was reaching with a naked finger for the buzzer beside the embassy's door when the security guard intercepted her.

'Young woman,' he said in Russian. 'What do you want?'

Instead of answering, she reached again for the button. The security man placed a glove on top of it. Olesya withdrew her finger and put her hand in her pocket.

'I said, what do you want?'

One bloodshot and one clear eye appraised her from beneath a beanie hat pulled low on his brow.

'Simon Davey, Mr Davey, he is the deputy ... deputy head of mission. I must ... I would like to see him. Please.'

'And who are you?' Her knees and thighs were grubby from her fall.

'Zarchenko, Olesya Zarchenko. Please.'

'Wait, please.'

She watched him retreat to the security hut at regulation pace, not slowly and not fast, a young man in a woollen hat, mildly overweight, somewhat pockmarked skin, torch and nightstick at his waist; another ordinary man, doing his job with the normal, desultory degree of exertion, mindlessly facilitating the end of the world. Through the rectangular window of the hut, as if framed by the aperture of a puppet theatre, he could be seen retrieving a sheaf of papers. He scanned the top sheet, flipped to the second, repeated the procedure.

She glanced at the buzzer. He was distracted by his papers. Two hours, three at the most. Two now, maybe less. She could push it. She should scream.

He regarded her through the window, then put down the papers and ambled back to the embassy's door.

'No. You're not on the list.'

'I know, I didn't say ... I don't have an appointment, I ...' She reached for the buzzer.

'No.'

'Please, it's an emergency. Just tell Simon, Mr Davey. Please.'

'I said, you're not on my list.' He sniffled, the mucus burbling in his nostrils. 'That's it.'

Two hours. One hour. They had left the barracks. They were in their buses. Curtains drawn, body armour on, visors down.

Truncheons ready. Guns loaded.

Guns.

'Please,' she said. 'Just call him.'

Water cannon. Armoured personnel carriers.

Guns.

She laid a hand on his hip. He looked down at the hand, and up again to interpret her face. His own face was blank.

Like a radio signal weakly reaching a stranded craft, she seemed to have contacted the human within him. Silently he returned to the hut and spoke into a walkie-talkie, monitoring her through the window. It was conceivable that a posse of his colleagues would materialise to drag her away. The guard finished speaking but remained inside the hut, watching. He nodded indecipherably.

A red light throbbed across the sky. Somebody fleeing, someone flying in from Moscow. Escape or attack. The rain had stopped.

The intercom crackled and a woman's voice addressed her. 'Zarchenko? Push the door, please.'

Constable and Turner prints hung on the walls of the meeting room. Low-slung armchairs formed a semicircle around a coffee table. Despite the hour the embassy was busy; people peered in from the corridor as they passed the open door. Iain, Jacqui, Lida the cook. Jacqui again.

'Not here,' Olesya said. 'It's secret.'

'What is it?'

He had met her in the lobby and escorted her through the metal detector and the inner security door. She had begun to hurry along the corridor, but he had called her back to the meeting room nearest the entrance.

'Please, no one else must hear, absolutely no one. Or they will ... Now, please. Now.'

'First, tell me what's going on.'

She glanced towards the door again. Quietly, she said, 'The square. If anybody knows what I say, I think ... I don't know what they do to me.'

He stroked his beard. 'There is a place, but I really shouldn't—'

'Please,' she said.

He covered his eyes, his neck and ears colouring as if he were holding his breath.

'Simon, I beg.'

'Come with me,' he whispered. 'Quickly.'

He marched along the corridor and she followed. They passed a staircase and several cubbyhole offices before arriving at another security barrier. Simon pressed his pass to a reader and opened it. Presently he halted at a keypad mounted beside a metal door. 'Leave your phone,' he told her.

She switched off her mobile, fumbling with the buttons, and placed it in a wooden rack. He punched in a code, opened the metal entrance and followed her through it. On the other side were a couple of yards of low-ceilinged corridor, like the airlock of a spaceship, and then another door. Simon reached around Olesya to the handle. She hesitated.

'Go on,' he urged. 'Go in.'

She stepped inside.

'I shouldn't,' Simon said, closing the last door, 'I really shouldn't ...'

'What is this place?'

She shivered. The filtered air in the box was cooler than the rest of the embassy. A teletype machine waited on a desk standing against the far wall.

'It's perfectly safe,' he said. 'You are. Metal's too thick for them to penetrate. Safest place in the embassy.'

She scanned the container-sized room. Grey hessian wallpaper hung on the metal walls; tired, cream-coloured linoleum disguised the metal floor. A set of spartan plastic chairs, such as you might find in a down-at-heel classroom, stood around a bare metallic conference table.

'Now,' he said. 'Tell me.'

'It's tonight.'

No windows. One entrance only. Nowhere to plant a bug.

'What is tonight, Olesya?' Sweat bloomed around the armpits of his shirt, in spite of the cold. 'We shouldn't be in here. My God.'

She tried to tame her breathing; she swallowed.

'Their attack is tonight.' She lowered her voice. 'Interior ministry troops. They have left their barracks, they are coming to the square. Soon they cross the river.'

'Hold on.'

'Now, two hours, I don't know,' she said, her voice rising again. 'Stop it. You must stop it.'

'Who told you this? Calm down.'

'Please. You know Andriy will never leave the square.' She touched Simon's forearm; he withdrew his other arm behind his back as if to protect it. 'You know it. Please.'

'Who told you, Olesya? Slowly.'

She released his arm. The strip lighting above them buzzed.

'It was ... It was the policeman. From our march, you remember, outside the presidential administration, I gave him my rose.'

'The young man? But this is ridiculous. How would he—'

'This man, with my rose, he has a cousin. His cousin calls him, he says—'

'What cousin? Really, I—'

'The cousin is in these barracks, interior ministry's. The cousin is coming. The man, my man, he knows I am from Ivano-Frankivsk. I told him. Yes. He came to the square, not in his uniform, in normal clothes. He came, he saw our banner, he recognises me. He says he feels pain for us; he says to get out, but quietly, no panic. Tell no one, never. So I come here, I come to you.'

Simon covered his mouth with a balled fist. The lights continued to buzz.

'With the greatest respect,' he said finally, 'there are always rumours. Precisely like this. Second-hand information, third-hand. Someone's uncle told them, a cousin told them. Every night since the tents went up, believe me. We cannot respond to every one. Our government, no government. Naturally.'

'It's not a rumour!' She controlled her voice, reducing it to a whisper. 'It's not. Andriy, he is my only ... My mother, I promised ... And Yaryna, if they will arrest her – her medicine, she needs it.'

'Olesya—'

'Every day she needs it. And they may not arrest – they may shoot. I swear you, only check.'

He shook his head.

'At least check. With the satellites. It's tonight, he said so. Check and you may stop it. You must.'

Her eyes were full but no tears escaped. Around her boots the floor was damp. She looked like a vision of grief from a myth, etched in sorrow, set to be transfigured into a tree or a rock.

'Olesya,' Simon repeated. 'You have to understand what you are asking. If we call the office – I mean London – they are likely to contact the Americans – that is, if they judge this to be credible – and if we're wrong, if you're wrong, they will be reluctant to listen to us again. I can see that you're distressed, but you have to be positive, do you see? Certain.'

'It's certain,' she said. 'Absolutely certain.'

For a few seconds he stared into her face. His eyes dimmed, as eyes do when a person is no longer looking outwards at all.

'Earlier today,' he said, 'this afternoon, outside the foreign ministry, I saw them snatch someone.' *Better your blood than theirs.* 'Wait here.'

'What are you going to do?'

'Speak to the ambassador. The ambassador first – her decision. Wait here.'

The church is near, but the way is icy.

Olesya sank, exhausted, to the hard floor. She undid her coat but drew in the lapels. She stood and paced around the table to the teletype machine. She held her skull in her hands and squeezed. Her phone was on the other side of the wall. She could not call Andriy, she could not warn Yaryna. She would have told them first but when she turned back in the colonnade Thibaut was watching her. She moved to the door of the box and grasped the handle, but released it.

She sat back on the floor, close to the door, like a dog waiting for its master; a young dog who fears its master will never return. She crossed her legs, resting her elbows on her knees as if she were practising yoga. The ceiling lights buzzed but no external sound penetrated the room. She raised her knees and clasped them to her chest. Her head fell back against the wall; the texture of the wallpaper was rough against her scalp.

Her grandmother told her, once, about the day the Germans came. The Soviets pulled out, burning and shooting, and some people thought the Germans would be better, if you had to choose. At the same time, they were scared. They waited. The odd thing was, her grandmother said, that her own memories of those hours, of the waiting, were serene. She was a child, it was summertime, and she and her friends ran into the forest. They hoped the Germans would never come and no one would be in charge. No more school. But they came, and after the waiting, everything was much worse.

The entry pad beeped. The internal door opened. No one entered but Olesya saw a woman's arm, pale fingers gripping the handle. The door began to close again, then halted and reopened a few inches, just enough for the woman to peer around the corner and verify what she thought she had seen.

It was Jacqui. The triumphant smile that had burst onto her face changed in quality when Olesya caught it, the spontaneous grin hardening into a rictus.

Olesya scrambled to her feet. 'Yes?'

Jacqui arched her eyebrows but said nothing. Before Olesya could speak again, she closed the door.

Olesya slumped back to the floor. Whereas, on the square, out in the open, the biting cold conquered her extremities but failed to penetrate her core, here, in the filtered air of the box, she was chilled to the bone. Chilled in her heart.

She recrossed her legs and waited.

The way is icy.

The door opened again and it was Simon. 'Just a sitrep,' he said. 'To let you know how things stand.'

She looked up at him from the floor. 'Please.'

'I briefed the ambassador. She notified the office; we believe they have spoken to Washington. We'll know more soon, so I suggest you … Just sit tight, my dear. If you can.'

He gave a hint of a smile, rocking nervily on his heels, as if to signify that there was more he wanted to say. Then he turned and left. The box was silent.

Forty minutes and an aeon later, the beeps sounded once more and the door reopened. Simon closed it behind him. 'Well,' he said. He stroked his beard. 'Well, well.'

Olesya rose from the floor. Her shoulders were hunched, her arms hung limp—the crumpled posture of the condemned. Simon sat down at the table, gingerly, like a man with a terrible hangover. But his face suggested an epiphany, eyes wide, lips round in amazement.

Olesya sat beside him and rested her hands on the table.

'Tell me again,' Simon said, 'who gave you this information.'

'As I said, the policeman.' They both stared down at the tabletop. 'From our march. My rose, he saw our banner …' She swallowed. 'Is it correct?' Above them, the light fitting buzzed. 'Is it happening?'

'They're safe,' Simon said, enjoining calm with the splayed fingers of his hand. 'For tonight, it's over. Perhaps altogether – after something like this, the regime may not recover. Terrible loss of face.'

Olesya glanced up at the buzzing as if searching for a wasp.

'It means it was real? The soldiers.'

'Yes, it was. They were.' He puffed out his cheeks. 'They were on their way, rather as you said. On the road from the airport, almost in the city. I will tell you what I can, but it must go no further, Olesya. You must never repeat this.'

She smiled almost invisibly; again the rigmarole of secrecy, this time without the threats. She nodded.

'The ambassador called the office, secure line in the comms room. She spoke to the regional director. I was with her – they asked for details, of course, the level of confidence. The source. One was ... I was economical with the truth. But I vouched for it.'

He stroked his beard. Olesya held her breath.

'London sent a flash telegram to our embassy in Washington. A flash ... that means urgent, more than urgent, like a war. It never happens. And Number 10 – our government – they called the Americans directly. One or two people in the State Department might remember me; that may have helped. In any case, they verified it – the troop movements. Satellites, human intel, informers, who knows? You were right.' He made a fist and brought it down onto the table, but softly. 'You were right. Two brigades of interior ministry troops had left their barracks. Seems the Kremlin has seen enough, they've been leaning on their friends here to get on with it.'

Olesya exhaled. She looked at the floor.

'The Americans were livid. They phoned the president – the old man, I mean, the outgoing president. Apparently he refused to take the call, even when it went up the food chain, you know, in Washington. The Secretary of State, I believe, but you mustn't ...'

'And what?'

'First the Americans did some hardballing, according to London. No visas for foreign travel, they implied, if the order wasn't rescinded. No holidays in the Algarve for any of them. No Côte d'Azur. Definitely no Miami Beach. That didn't go down well, apparently. *Lèse-majesté*. You know, disrespect.'

'But our government accepts? It does what they ask?'

'Not immediately. They claimed the Americans had been misinformed – it's rats in a sack in the administration, they're panicking, quite possibly the president had nothing to do with the orders. So Washington did some sweet-talking as well. Sketched the dignified retirement that awaited if they hit the brakes. Made assurances about the official yacht, London said. And the state dacha – the blasted state dacha.'

'What about the dacha?

'That no one would take it away, whatever happens next. The Americans said they could see to that, they gave their word. Very basic, really, what things come down to in the end. What life comes down to. Life and death. A dacha and a yacht.'

'It's clear.' The buzzing seemed to have stopped. 'And?'

'They still denied it all, over in Bankova. They denied that any orders had been given, denied that any troops had been deployed. But they said that they would look into it – for the sake of the country's reputation, you understand. They promised nothing, they admitted nothing, but they would look into it. Some flannel about how they had always valued good relations.'

Simon patted the table with both hands. He smiled.

'And they did?' Olesya said quietly. 'They stopped it?'

'Apparently one of the brigades had already turned back. Seems the officer had disobeyed – call of conscience, halted his men on their way into town. Quite heroic, really. The other – they were coming. It was real.' At this, Olesya gave a short, strangulated moan. 'But somebody up there stopped it, yes – didn't want to answer for the blood. Very clear on the satellite, London said. Five minutes after the last phone call, the troops pull in at the side of the road. Five minutes after that, they turn around and go home. Of course the old gang will say this never happened now. And someone'll have to explain to the Russians why they didn't go through with it. Won't be at all pleased up in Moscow.'

He leaned towards her. 'Well done.'

She turned away from him and put a hand over her mouth.

'You must never ...' he said. 'Neither of us can talk about this now, it's confidential.'

'I understand.'

For a long moment they sat in silence. At last Simon rose from the table. 'You really ought not to be in here,' he said. 'My fault, of course. In the circumstances, I thought ... You'll have to go now. Will you manage?'

'Yes,' she said. 'I may.' She buttoned her coat.

'Just a second,' Simon said. 'Wait a second.'

He opened the door, passed through the airlock and peered along the corridor.

'Quickly, please,' he said, holding the doors open for her, one with each hand. She ducked under his arm and retrieved her phone from the rack. He led her back through the security doors and towards the front of the embassy. He paused when they reached reception.

'This is not the time, Olesya, but one has to say, you did the right thing tonight. A situation like that, the presence of mind ...'

'Thank you, Mr Davey. Simon.'

Voices emanated from the meeting room, a man and a woman. As Simon glanced towards the open door, Olesya stepped forward and embraced him. His body tensed, his arms by his sides and unresponsive, but he relented. She pressed her head against his shoulder; his hand swept upwards to stroke her hair. He closed his eyes.

'Thank you,' she repeated. He patted her back, resting his hand between her shoulder blades.

She disentangled herself and smoothed her hair. 'So,' she said, 'I will go down.'

'Yes, do.'

She put on her hat and mittens.

'Remember,' he said, 'it's terribly important, all of this has only just happened, it's strictly between us, you can't—'

'It's clear.'

He saw her to the front door. Outside, the security man was in his hut; he glanced up when she emerged, but not for long.

'We thank you,' she said again to Simon as she stepped into the cold. He gave a brisk, shoulder-height wave, like an abortive salute, and closed the embassy's door.

She smiled at the guards outside the ministry as she headed for Independence Square. Ordinary men; harmless men. Protesters were trickling through the monastery's gates to thaw out inside. The night sky was overcast but luminous, as if a fire were burning beyond the mesh of clouds. As she turned onto Mykhailivska Street, her phone rang.

'Yes?' She walked on, taking short, scuffed steps on the slippery descent.

'It's Thibaut, Mr Kovrin's—'

'Yes, I know you.'

She halted on the pavement outside a *varenichnaya*, her breath glistening in the light from inside. The tables and the stools at the counter were empty.

'Mr Kovrin wanted ... Who did you tell?'

'Nobody.' Inside the café, beneath a scribbled menu board offering cherry and potato *vareniki*, the old woman behind the counter smiled at her. With her grey bun, apron and apple-round face, she resembled Olesya's grandmother. 'Only who you said,' she assured Thibaut, smiling back at the old woman. 'Only him.'

'Somebody talked, though. You can see it on the square.'

'What's on the square? Who's there?' The *babusia* in the cafe frowned in sympathy with her expression.

'Not the attack, not that – it's just that they're scared there, they're getting ready. It could be the security service told them something. They're making barricades.'

'It wasn't me, I told only at the embassy, only what you said. Only him, I swear.'

A hand muffled the phone at Thibaut's end; words were exchanged that came through as blurs, like the Morse pulses of whales.

'What did he say? At the embassy.'

'It was true. It was real. But just now they stopped it.'

'Who?'

'I'm not supposed ... He said I mustn't ... Isn't this enough?'

'Who was it? Mr Kovrin is waiting.'

She hesitated. She met the old woman's gaze. The old woman nodded, or seemed to.

'The Americans. He said the Russians wanted troops to come but the Americans stopped them. They pressed our old government, the soldiers were called back.'

Another indecipherable exchange, up in their office near the opera house or out in the annexe behind the silent fountain.

'Thank you,' Thibaut said. 'We thank you.'

He hung up. She looked again for the old woman but the counter was vacant. She must have gone into the kitchen. Olesya pulled her hat down over her ears.

At the bottom of the hill, people were carrying tyres and benches, rubbish bins and bollards, heaving them above their heads or lugging them in teams. They looked like survivors salvaging possessions from a flood. Olesya was behind the stage and could not see the screen, but the speaker was familiar. The candidate with the ruined face was talking fast, beseeching those listening at home to reinforce the protest while there was still time. 'Come to the square, brothers! Tonight!' His voice was scratchy, giving out. 'They are trying to bring us to our knees! Come tonight!'

So he knew. But he didn't know. In the crush Olesya was lifted off her feet, and for a few seconds seemed destined to be trampled. Instead the benign organism deposited her on the road, safe, the safest person in the city, the most serene where recently she had been the most frantic, because she alone knew that the danger had been averted. They were piling up the debris at the edge of Independence Square and around the monument, an improvised barricade that she knew they would not need. The old man would keep his dacha and she would keep her brother. She did not feel cold, not at all.

She registered the Ivano-Frankivsk banner, still flying in front of the Conservatory, and shouldered her way towards her friends.

vi. The lion

WIN-WIN outcomes: that is what the office taught us to pursue. Resist zero-sum thinking, they told us. Reason our adversaries into partnership. Promote our partners to allies. The best of all possible worlds.

Daydreams. *Bullshit.* Winners mean losers, just as Kovrin avers.

'It's good of you to spare the time,' I say to him, the old diplomatese reflexively kicking in.

He shrugs. 'Sorry to say, is only for few minutes. So, tell me what is the reason, Simon? For pleasure of our visit.'

Simon – the name of an expendable contact from over a decade ago. I imagine his memory is a substantial part of his success, a Rolodex of grudges, weaknesses, blackmailable secrets. A scientific habit of mind that he likely acquired on a chemistry course in a Soviet institute in the olden days. And, alongside it, a coercive kind of charm that one watches in operation – as if from under an anaesthetic, locked in – yet finds impossible to resist.

'That night, in Kiev, all those years ago – you were behind it all, Mr Kovrin. You set up the whole thing.'

'Yes.'

'What?'

'Yes, this happened. We did this. And so?'

I was expecting a lie, perhaps one of his translucent lies, like deep but clear water, the truth resting somewhere at the bottom, refracted yet visible if one knows how to look for it.

'The leak about the attack on the square and the Americans – even the warning we were given in the first place ...' To protect Olesya, I entwine what she told me with my guesswork. 'It all came from you, didn't it?'

'Absolutely. This is a fact.'

'You ruined me, Mr Kovrin.'

He shrugs again. 'Is cost of business.'

This is what I wanted, of course: a confession. For my replacement grudge. Still, his failure to dissemble is obscurely insulting. He returns to his computer – something amusing is displayed on the screen, I gather, because he is grinning. Unless, on the contrary, the amusing thing is me.

... *information which has been communicated in confidence within Government or received in confidence from others* ...

'If I may, though: why? Why did you do this to me?'

'To you?' he scoffs. 'Is not to you. Not personal. We try for compromise, but no, no deal – you remember in Saint Sophia's, how I try? – and straight away our government sends these soldiers. If they attack, if I let them, people will be killed. If people is killed, not one but hundreds, is disaster for everybody. Blood means not only blood. Means sanctions, absolutely – banking sanctions, stock exchange, travel ban. We see this now, is a fact. Blood is worst solution. So, I try to stop.'

'Except it wasn't you. If my supposition is correct, you sent—'

He raises a hand. 'But trying is not same as doing. Maybe it stops. Maybe it goes on – the soldiers in the square. Means I must be careful. Maybe they can win still, our old government. So must nobody know it comes from me, this warning that we send you. Nobody – not then, not afterwards. It must come from somebody else.'

'So you sent her. The girl.'

I never entirely believed the story of the riot policeman with the rose. Grand romantic gesture. Improbable.

He cocks his head in confirmation. He smiles. Perhaps he no longer much cares about this crisis of the *ancien régime*. Altogether too much water under the bridge for it, or me, to matter to him now. Too much blood.

'We have plan B on that night, if I remember, in case you will not see her. We had an army general, tame one, we will send him to the Americans instead. But she was our most efficient way.'

He drums his fingers on the desk. I sense my time is running out.

'Understood. But, if I may, you stopped it, they turned back – wasn't that enough? Why not keep it to yourself?'

A derisive snort. 'This is why you are not businessman, Simon. To waste something of value? This information – new information – about the Americans, their phone calls, what the girl tells us, this is something valuable. Very. Something to trade.'

'Trade with whom?'

Again he raises his hand, soliciting patience like a traffic policeman at a crossroads.

'After that night,' he says, 'government is finished, that is a fact. Like a bear, when he runs away. Like communists with their tanks in Moscow. Soldiers say no, Americans say no, soldiers go home, is finished. They lose, no second chances. So I trade. With winners. I tell them – this Vlasych, I know her already, we speak, me and she, we understand each other – I tell her not all, but enough.' He leans forward conspiratorially. 'You've seen her – Vlasych – she tells you something maybe? Somebody from her team?'

Straight-faced, I neither confirm nor deny. 'She's back in America, I believe.'

He grunts. 'In any cases, is normal, what she did. Like animals at the zoo. Take turns at their food, then time to go.'

We were playing the wrong game, I recall Vlasych telling us at the embassy. She was right, in a way. National interest, enduring values, all those old-fashioned considerations – they were for the birds, I now see. Money – that, evidently, was what swung it on Independence Square. I had thought there was some nobility mixed in, but it was just money.

'So you switched sides? Just like that.' I click my fingers clumsily. 'After all your efforts on their behalf, the meetings we had, all your threats – you betrayed them, your pals in the old regime. You sold them out.'

'Is not betrayed.' He raises his voice, such that I glance involuntarily at the security camera. Kovrin clocks the gesture and smiles. 'This is bullshit,' he says. 'Is not sides, absolutely not. Betrayed! Is like gravity, law of nature. You read Hemingway?'

'Excuse me?'

'Hemingway. For me, is number one from the Americans. You know his Spanish story? For me, is his best. In this story, the man, the fighter, at the end, he tells his girl, he explains, what is best place in line when they ride into open, when there will be shooting, riding horses across this road. You remember? He explains to the girl – he loves his girl – he says first in line is okay, they are not expecting you, your enemy. Second is best. But not last – they kill you. Don't be last across this road. You remember?'

'Vaguely.' I never liked Hemingway. Macho nonsense, in my view.

'Here is same story, more or less. In this situation – power is changing, or maybe it is changing, no one can say – first is not so good. Do not cross first to opposition. First is bad horse. Maybe nobody comes behind, could be revolution fails. First is too much risk.' He uncurls and wags a single finger. 'After, is okay. Second. Third.' Two fingers, three. 'But not last. To switch last to opposition side, there is no prizes. From my point of view, it's like gravity. The change is starting slow, then fast, then faster faster faster. Last means to be crushed. Last is dead.'

He balls a fist and grinds it into his other palm. 'Means big question is timing. Don't be first – too much risk. Don't be last – crushed. So when? For me, this was when. That night, these soldiers. My information. You fight and you fight and then, at certain point, you jump.'

His hand describes an arc above his desk. 'You jump,' Kovrin reiterates. 'To keep what is yours, you jump. So, I tell Vlasych, Vlasych tells world. Everyone knows, government power is gone. Every soldier, he knows do not obey. For me, information means points. Points in bank with new government, and not only points. Afterwards, they remember, and what is mine, I keep. I told you maybe this saying, my favourite: *My friend is near to me, but my belly is nearer.*'

I thought this man would ferry me to an ambassadorship. I thought he was my master stroke. It was like the old parable, in which the scorpion is bound in the end to sting.

'Yes, I see the choreography now. Your logic. Very efficient, as you might say.'

What would happen, I wonder, if I were to lurch from this chair and across the desk and grab him by the throat and squeeze? Possibly he will press a button and the troll will burst in. The arm behind the back again, and worse. Naturally there is the camera, too. The camera would be enough to mobilise his men.

'One more thing,' he says. 'Final thing. Off records? He is not my friend, this old man, our old president. Not real friend. I know people say this' – he raises his palms again, hunching in his shoulders – 'and at one time it was useful to me, this idea, maybe it was useful to him. But is not true. You know this famous story, about lion in the apartment?'

'I don't believe I do.'

If there is one thing I have learned today, conclusively, it is that there is no violence in me after all. The mettle required to act – I find I still have that. But not violence.

'You don't know this story? A man keeps his lion in his apartment. It's Soviet apartment – small. Circus man. His neighbours say him, take this lion out, lions is dangerous, he will eat you. Man says, lion is my friend, I know this lion, my pet since he is a baby. He feeds his lion, they sleep together. They walk together in their park. You know what happens to him?'

'I don't. But I imagine you'll tell me.' Aesop in a *kommunalka*.

'He eats this man. In the ends, his lion eats him. So – nasty story. But good lesson. Friends with the creature who can eat you, it's dangerous. Same for businessman and power.

Don't be too close. Close enough, but not too close. The lion eats him.'

Kovrin is beaming. One can see that he considers this Solomonic wisdom. Perhaps it is. Behind him, the river and the sky are a mauvish grey.

'Quite,' I say. 'And I see the choice you faced. The momentum on the square, your concern for your businesses – your belly, as you put it. But I don't see why, afterwards, you dragged me into it. Me personally, Mr Kovrin. Misha. All the stuff in the newspapers about the girl and me, my marriage.'

'What are you talking about?'

The door opens and Natalia Kovrina comes in. She takes three paces towards her husband and stands with her arms by her sides. She was once an air stewardess, as I recall, that is said to be how they met. She looks rather as if she is poised to give a safety presentation.

'A word, please,' she says in Russian.

'Go on,' Kovrin says.

'You're busy.' She glances towards me.

You should pay your cleaner more, I think. *Your husband keeps an apartment on Baseina Street.*

'It's not important,' Kovrin says. *I'm* not important, in other words.

She pauses. A slight grimace.

'It's Nikita. He wants to go to Paris, he wants to take the Mercedes.'

'And what?'

'Should I send Timur with him?'

Kovrin's fingers drum the desk. His eyes dart towards the computer screen. 'Okay,' he says. 'Send him. That's all?'

'Yes.' She regards him coldly, nods and leaves. Often I have wondered whether, had we survived, Cynthia and I would eventually have settled into an arrangement like this one, somewhat more suburban, *sans* Mercedes and bodyguards, her eyeing me contemptuously as I slurp my soup on our ill-advised restaurant forays. Especially after Nancy fluttered off to university and into her own life. I picture us sitting in silence on a sofa, in whichever Home Counties town we retired to – nothing left to talk about, like most couples, one supposes, when they outlive the realistic life expectancy of their affection. This vision offers a perverse form of comfort, albeit camouflaged as masochism: the reassurance that, in the long run, there would have been nothing much to lose and thus, from a certain perspective, nothing was or could have been lost.

'Is a season in this,' Kovrin says. 'I mean, for our time in London. Is a season in all things, yes? Like Bible says. Sometimes I am not here, absolutely not at all, house is all for her. Now, with tricky situation in Kiev, new vectors in administration – here I am, but she is not expecting me.' He shrugs. 'Last thing, anyway, before you go. I am sure you are busy man. This girl, you said?'

Deep breath. Count to ten. She used to confide in Lida, the embassy cook, I found out afterwards – Cynthia did. Cried on her shoulder in the kitchen. *More time for me than you ever had*, apparently.

I say, 'The story about the girl and me, it wasn't even true. In the paper. It was true that I was involved that night, you know that. But the rest of it was lies.'

Kovrin hesitates. I can see the ratiocination behind his eyes, the gears clicking, the calculator whirring, intuiting whether anything much is to be won or lost. Instant arbitrage. Not a procedure that he normally conducts in public, I'd wager, like the secret habit of an exotic animal. 'For this,' he says finally, 'I cannot help you.'

'The newspapers,' I reiterate. 'All the sleazy business about the girl, the idea that she and I, that we ... It cost me my job. Not just my job.'

He turns towards his computer again but I do not think he is focusing on it. He is stalling.

'That was not us,' he says. He makes another pacifying gesture with his hands, palms out. 'I remember this, something like this, yes. But it was not us. Not me.'

'Thibaut, then. Your man.'

'From my point of view, why do this? We get to know each other, me and you, we understand each other. We like each other – maybe we like each other. This for me is an investment. Why should I write it off? Also, now, after the square, I know something about you, something new, this role you play for us, our joint venture, so to say. One day this can be useful.' He winks. I swallow. 'Something else to trade. Why would I give away for nothing? Bullshit! For what?'

I see his point. I thought he may have wanted me out of the way, off the scene, as one might – as quite possibly he might – rub out a witness to an assassination. But, yes, I could indeed have been more useful to him *in situ*, compromised and pliable.

What I say is: 'Why should I believe you?'

Kovrin swats a hand. 'Believe, don't believe, this is not important. We are not angels, frankly speaking. Not absolutely clean. Not pure white. But this, we did not do. No. We say ... What is it we say? This thing you say always in your leaks ... "Western diplomat". Yes. We say "Western diplomat" tells us about these soldiers who turn back, about the Americans. That is what we tell Vlasych, nothing else. Nothing about Simon Davey and his girl.'

Two planks of scaffold removed in a single day and nothing to replace them. It wasn't Olesya who undid me. It wasn't Kovrin. Or rather, it was not only Olesya and Kovrin.

'Do you know who it was?'

'*Nyet.*'

I stroke my beard. Through the window, atop a pylon, a lone red light flashes above the river and the trees.

'What is your situation now?' he asks me. 'If it is not secret.'

'Sorry?'

'Your situation. You are ... in difficulties?'

For me, the calculation is easy. Probably no benefit to confiding in this man, but no conceivable cost.

'Since you ask, I have been better, yes.'

'You are working? To live. To eat.'

'In a manner of speaking.' I look at my shoes. 'I drive. Taxi apps and so on. Just sometimes, for pocket money. While I wait for my pension.'

The foreign drivers have it worse. Muttered xenophobia, and moreover, one senses, the ubiquitous implication that they must not know what they are doing or where they are going. But we indigenous drivers can suffer, too. The pity – it is written on the passengers' faces, as if they were bystanders at a minor tragedy. They hear the pukka accent and the pity blossoms. Then they sigh over the route and look at their phones.

Once again, I do not mention the drinking. In any case the drinking is in the past, no longer etched in pointillist scarlet on my cheeks and nose. Stains around my trouser flies. Unaccountable bruises.

'I remember, you had one daughter. Is it right?'

That steel-trap, blackmail-ready memory.

'It is, but we're not in touch. Not regularly.' I am not certain for whom I add this proviso. Not regularly and not ever. We are never in touch: that is the truth.

'Children!' Kovrin says. 'Impossible! The Mercedes! You hear this?' He wags a finger at the spot where his wife had stood. 'Absolutely impossible!'

'So I gather.'

'It is sad,' Kovrin says, averting his eyes. 'Sad story.' He says this as if my biography were an actual story, fiction, like Hemingway, not the chronicle of a real person's life, a life currently being lived on the other side of his desk. I glimpse the grey hair patterning his temple. He clicks his tongue.

'You want I should help you?'

His hands are poised on the keyboard but they do not type. This, I was not anticipating. First Olesya with her offer to write to Nancy, now Kovrin – two unexpected kindnesses in a single afternoon.

'I'm not altogether sure if that would be … appropriate. Ethically, I mean. But thank you for the thought.'

Do not knowingly take a favour from the scorpion – one of Olesya's grandmother's mottos, as I recall. Advice that poor Olesya herself was not able to follow.

'Is possible,' he says. 'Absolutely possible.'

I envisage the cage they put me in, not long ago, in his basement. I could be his cage-sweeper. His messenger boy. Or, one supposes, his procurer.

'Means in foundation,' he says. 'Conservation work, the orphanages, our libraries. On my board is three lords. No, two lords, three sirs. One MP. It can be here, it can be in Paris – there are variants.'

... your behaviour, action or inaction must not significantly disrupt or damage the performance or reputation of the Diplomatic Service ...

From a certain angle, taking Kovrin's shilling would be an exquisite form of revenge against the office. Poetic justice, as it were, disreputable conduct after the fact. They wouldn't like it, not a bit, but there is not much more that they could do to me.

Yet I baulk. My pride has not been entirely extinguished – another of today's discoveries. 'With the best will in the world,' I say, 'I'm not sure, at my age—'

'Okay.' Kovrin mimes washing his hands, slap-slap. 'Conscience is clear,' he says, as if one's morality were an asset one could pawn for a year, a decade, and then buy back at a convenient moment, at a discount haggled out with one's past. 'I try.'

I must acknowledge the possibility that Kovrin has changed. He was a brute to Olesya in Kiev, that much is clear, but there can be no furtive reason for him to make this offer. People do change, nothing stays the same, not over a decade, whether one spends it in Donetsk or Disney World.

'Very kind,' I mumble. 'Truly.'

I should also admit the possibility that Kovrin was never what I presumed him to be. Or, not entirely. Not exclusively. A person is always more than his reputation. Or less. If people seem unpredictable, if they surprise us, it may be because we did not attend to them sufficiently in the first place.

'Only this, then,' he says. He has braced his forearms against the arms of his chair as if he were preparing to rise and leave. 'This much, only. Little help, only.' With a thumb and forefinger he makes a diminutive gesture that I dimly recognise. 'Don't worry,' he says, 'you can take this, no conflict of interest. Advice only, no need to declare.'

'I'm listening,' I say, transported, momentarily, back to that winter, the gazebo on his estate, the cathedral. 'Give me your advice.'

Who was it? My nemesis in the newspapers. Not Olesya. Not Kovrin.

'Simply this,' he expounds. 'Any situation – I mean new situation – the secret, main key, is speed of adapting. Fastest to adapt is one who wins. You understand? Is only thing you control. New government, new business, new partners. New country. New wife.' He grins. 'Rich, poor. Happy, not happy. Prison, free. Adapt.'

I do not recall hearing that Kovrin had ever been in prison, but no doubt it was possible. Not infrequently there were rumours of a bigwig having been incarcerated at the fag end of communism or – having failed to pay off the right officials or trespassed on a better-connected gangster's turf – during the free-for-all years that followed. Rumours that were impossible to substantiate because the paperwork had been destroyed, and no one involved was inclined to reminisce.

'I think,' Kovrin continues, hands now clasped on his desk, thumbs twiddling like a hamster wheel, 'is advantage of our history. Is many disadvantages, but this is one advantage. To adapt. Absolutely. Russians come, Poles come. Once upon the time, Mongols. Germans come, more than once. Tatars. Litvaks. They come, they fight, is like boxing ring for world. Someone wins, we adapt. They give our cities new names, okay, these are names. They make new rules, okay, these are rules. New money, okay, we use this money, here is some.' He mimes paying a bribe. 'But in your country, with the great respect' – he smiles – 'just one little bump, like this Europe vote you made, and everyone is fainting. Everyone is screaming. End of world! Help! Call police! This is big disadvantage.'

'You know, you may be onto something there. Quite intemperate, the whole thing.'

'Is a fact. Your life now, you must to adapt – not accept, adapt. Make something new where you are, stop thinking only where you were before.'

Prison? Poverty? Those childhood years in the *kommunalka*, I suppose. Men like him lead multiple lives. 'Very stoical,' I say. 'Like Epictetus.'

'We must eat lemon to understand sugar. That is what they say, our *babushkas*. This, I do not agree, is better always sugar. But if you have only lemons – best is to like lemons. Suck. Enjoy. You understand? If you have only *kasha*, eat the *kasha*. Or you starve.'

Easy for you to say, I think. But what I say is, 'Definitely food for thought, Mr Kovrin. I will give that a whirl.'

'This trouble now at home – the revolution, the East. Tanks. War. You think this is problem? Nineties, that was problem. Bombs. Shooting. Raiders. Still, you adapt. To defend your businesses. Your honour. Your businesses. For myself, in nineties, I would prefer to find another way, but sometimes if there is no choice, with raiders, when it is necessary, I—'

*

181

There is a knock at the door. It opens and a man enters. Not the arm-twister, not the troll, another man. Not Thibaut. Rimless glasses, navy suit, no tie. Noiseless footsteps, like a burglar. He must see me but does not acknowledge my presence, as if I were a mistress whom it was politic not to register. I notice an elephant-foot wastepaper bin beneath Kovrin's desk.

'Mr Kovrin,' he says. He is holding an iPad, dug horizontally into his waist. 'New York, I've set it up next door. It's coming up for eight-thirty.'

Not Thibaut, but cut from the same cloth: the newsreader teeth, the high-class servility, the elusive continental accent. Swedish, I fancy, possibly Danish.

'Absolutely,' Kovrin says. 'We finish now. Give me five minutes, okay?'

'Of course.'

The man folds the iPad's cover over the screen. He remains where he is for a beat longer than seems suitable, a momentary assertion of independence, before he retreats. He closes the door. I expect Kovrin to shoo me out, but instead he turns on the television mounted on the wall behind me. An American voice interprets the stock and commodity prices that flicker in esoteric columns on the screen.

'Your other man,' I say. 'Thibaut. What happened to him?'

Kovrin lowers the volume on the television with the remote control. 'The Swiss? He was ... Thibaut ... He was set free.'

He droops his mouth, bobbing his head as if in condolence. He picks at something between his teeth with the nail of a little finger.

'Okay,' he says. 'So.' A tiny flap of both hands, like a conductor's *pianissimo*, signifies the end.

'If I may,' I venture, 'one last question.'

'Absolutely final.'

I clear my throat. 'Why don't you just leave? I mean, why don't you sell up, take your winnings, settle down here or on Capri or—'

'Capri, I sold. Mistake, maybe.'

'All the same, I find it baffling. Why run all these risks? All of this – the bodyguards, that cage in your basement.'

Kovrin has a new expression on his face, one I have not seen before. Not insulted, not alarmed. Confounded. As if I had suggested that the Earth was flat, and orbited by the sun.

He shakes his head. 'Is against rules,' he says. 'Rules of the game. No checking out, is not possible. Means you lose.'

'But, if I may, you gamble' – there is no way to put this delicately – 'well, you gamble with your life over there. With prison, or even worse.'

Car bombs, drive-bys: they seem to flare up every other week these days, so the World Service informs me, eliminating some gangster-oligarch or other.

'Is safer inside,' he says. 'This is your mistake. Safer inside the game. To leave, makes no difference, nobody forgets, they find you always. Inside, you have something to trade. Anyway, we always gamble, no? Life is all gamble. To breathe is even to gamble.' He exhales dramatically, puffing out his cheeks, a tang of coffee on his breath. 'You gambled, no? You gamble on revolution. On the square. You try for big prize, you lose.'

I bridle at this equivalence. 'That wasn't for myself,' I tell him. 'It isn't the same thing.'

He laughs, a short, hard, artillery-shell guffaw.

'Typical,' Kovrin says. He rises from his throne. His hands smooth the outside pockets of his jacket as if he were checking for his keys. 'Not for yourself? Absolutely typical. I know what you are thinking. You think I am dirty, yes? My money. Muddy. You think in your country, money is different, money has no smell. Nice cup of tea, nice little job, only good things, do no harm. Like in cinema, Jimmy Stewart – you think you are Jimmy Stewart, Hollywood hero. I must to tell you, this does not exist.' He reaches for the remote and switches off the TV. 'All money smells, you understand? Clean money, nice cup of tea – in my country, this option does not exist. From my point of view, does not exist here also. You think so, but is bullshit. Fairy tale. Better perfume only. Now.'

I stand up too. This is doubtless the last time we will see one another.

'This business on the square,' he continues, 'this was not for you? Nothing there for you, only for others? Fairy tale!'

Again the howitzer guffaw. He is right, of course. I did anticipate a reward, albeit not a pecuniary one. Honour, promotion – a different kind of currency, but a currency all the same.

'Money is always muddy,' I summarise, 'so everything is allowed, is that it? All the corruption. The privatisations.' I place a hand on his desk.

'Only secondary market,' he says on autopilot. 'Market prices.'

'No one is an angel, so you can steal whatever you like. Is that what you're saying, Misha?'

He picks up a quartz paperweight, tosses it in his palm and gently puts it down again. 'If it is not me,' he says, 'is someone else. Is like weather. Rain. Not something you will change. You can change only whether you take umbrella.' He straightens his lapels. 'All these slogans, rule of law, democracy – this at time being is our ambition. Is like communism, you remember? We were not good enough for purest communism, it was a slogan only. Same now with rule of law – one day we can have it, when judges are ready, police. Politicians. But not yet.'

Kovrin comes around the desk and heads for the door. I follow him. He turns and grips my shoulder.

'In the ends,' he says, 'we were like sign to future, no? Our little country. This election, the square. Like Yuri Gagarin. They sent their political technologists – the Kremlin sent them to us first. The phony TV, money for demonstrations, all these rumours. They sent them to us, then by internet around the world. To America, your country, here. It was experiment, I think. We were pioneers. It failed, but they thought, no, is good plan, we try harder. So they tried. Now it's everywhere, this technology. Paid protests, paid everything.'

'On that score,' I concede, 'I fear you may well be right.' These days we are all lost in the labyrinth of rumour, too discombobulated to find our way out, or looking up at a screen on which we see projected images of ourselves.

He is clasping the door handle when he turns again. 'She is here, you know.'

I swallow, involuntarily. 'Who?' I avoid his eyes, as no doubt he notices.

'That little one, this girl we send to you. Not a girl now. Your friend, or ... your friend.'

'Where?'

185

'In London. Here, in this house. Two, three times each week, she helps our housekeeper. I see her sometimes, absolutely. You did not know this already?'

Do not look at him, I tell myself. Conceivably this faux-casual last-ditch inquiry is, for Kovrin, the real point of our conversation – all the homilies on history, the lion and the rest being so much misdirection to lull me into unmasking my source.

'No,' I say. I sense my mouth drying. *On my honour.* 'It's a long time since we've been in touch. What a strange coincidence.'

'Not coincidence,' Kovrin says. I focus on a point over his shoulder, on the oak-panelled door. The spy hole. 'We bring her here – for nanny, cleaning. It was good to keep her close, after what she does for us. She was living here before, top floor, quiet … But nowadays it's not so important to have her – all this was long ago, too much more happened to us since then. Anyway, we trust her, she knows to stay quiet. Like I trust you.'

I take the hint and nod.

'A good girl,' he says. 'Good to her family. She has spirits.'

Saying nothing about Olesya, I realise, a total absence of curiosity, is liable to be incriminating as well.

'I had not thought the two of you … You were on opposite sides, after all. Apart from that night.'

'Is not sides, is people! All sides is made from people. She and I, we came to understanding. I try to help her, like I try to help you.'

In Kiev they call it sponsorship. 'Well, give her my regards.'

'Absolutely,' he says.

He opens the door. The troll is standing on the other side. I surmise that he has been there throughout. Momentarily I think I am heading back to the cage.

Kovrin says, 'Timur will see you out.'

He walks across the hallway and through another door, beyond which I can see a wall-mounted screen displaying an image of a conference table. He does not glance over his shoulder or say goodbye or shake my clammy hand. His assistant closes the door behind him.

Timur raises an arm and I flinch. 'Yours,' he says. On his broad palm lie my keys, wallet and phone. My swimming bag dangles from his wrist, the strings indenting his hairy skin. He bites his nails, I notice.

'Thank you.'

'It's nothing. Please.' He extends an arm to indicate the front door. I follow him past the polo-mint sculpture and the ebony figurine. The alarm system beeps. He leads me across the threshold and down the steps. On this side of the garden wall is a border of flowers that is not visible from the street, lovely if somewhat garish. From the path one cannot see the pavement or the asphalt, only the river, the trees on the opposite bank and the sky. All dark.

Explanations are a type of restitution, are they not? Albeit a phantom kind. If we can fathom why something happened, decipher who, finally, was to blame, where the misstep occurred, we imagine we might somehow go back and correct it. Time travel, make-believe, but better than nothing. A powerful urge – now destined, in my case, to remain unrequited.

Timur opens the gate. He stands beneath the climbing roses.

'You're okay?' he asks. 'Your arm.'

'Yes. Thank you,' I find myself saying.

'Okay,' he says. 'Good luck.'

He has kind eyes. I offer him a no-hard-feelings smile and step through the gate and onto the towpath.

7. The embankment

3 December

INSTINCTIVELY they kept together when they left the embassy, like penguins shuffling across the tundra. As they passed St. Andrew's church, and began the twisty descent, they separated into a straggling column. A gaggle of first and second secretaries formed the vanguard, walking in the road and joking with the local staff, young women in high heels on which they magically negotiated the cobbles. Cynthia was at the rear, in line with the ambassador, the economic counsellor's husband and the political counsellor's wife. Simon was in the middle, awkward on the ice, oscillating between the road and the hazardously smooth pavement. Ahead of him the ambassador's husband slipped, flailing on the spot like a slapstick comedian until Iain took his arm.

'Little steps,' Iain said. 'Like in rugby.' He was wearing felt winter boots and an Astrakhan hat. 'Good lad.'

The theatre on the slope was closed. They passed a stall selling keyrings, snow globes and fridge magnets, laid out for tourists whom the revolution had scared off. Warily, the ambassador's husband scuffed his boots across the sheen. Jacqui had been delayed in the office, promising to catch them up.

Halfway down, Iain slowed his pace, taking purposefully tiny strides like a child playing *What's the time, Mr Wolf?* He materialised at Simon's shoulder.

'Death of us, this slope. More dangerous than the riot police. Absolute death.'

'I couldn't agree more. Strong case for taxis in my opinion. But.'

'Your wife all right, is she?'

Simon looked up from the ground and paused. 'Thank you, she's fine.'

Iain cleared his throat. 'It's pretty hairy,' he said. 'The aggro.'

'So I gather,' Simon said. 'The former interior minister, chap who came to our party? Shot himself in the head, apparently. In his *banya*, I expect you heard. Suicide, according to the official verdict, only he seems to have shot himself twice – twice in the head. He was mixed up in that murder, the reporter they found in the forest. Evidently knew too much.'

'Poor chap,' Iain said. 'But that's not what I'm talking about. It's the Americans. I'm talking about the Americans.'

Involuntarily Simon glanced back over his shoulder towards the embassy, the ambassador, the illuminated church looming like a lighthouse on the bluff above them. The church is near, but the way is icy.

'They're spitting,' Iain continued, 'over there in Kotsubinsky. My pal Brent from security called me this afternoon. Fucker was absolutely spitting – he's CIA, probably, I don't know. Watch that ice patch … There … I said to him, "Brent, you had to expect this to leak, no? How many fuckers do you think knew about it? Hell, you wanted it to leak, I expect." He's having none of it, Brent. CIA guy, you know the sort.' Simon kept his eyes fixed on the cobbles. 'Throat-slitting, sure, be my guest. Leaks, no. No way. Preppy assassin type, you know. Wants to know who it was told the radio station about their telephone ping-pong, the way they nixed the attack, all that. Says it weakens their hand, next fucker in Whereverstan won't trust them to keep shtum when they try to winkle him out. Witch hunt over there, I'm hearing. He's hanging everyone up by their ankles.'

'Charming.'

'Isn't it?'

They fell silent. Laughter resounded in front of them – *It's not possible!* a woman's voice protested – spasmodic pleasantries to their rear.

'That one there,' Simon said. 'No, that one.' He indicated a yellow and white pre-revolutionary mansion. 'That was Bulgakov's house, you know.'

'Yes.'

'You know, from *The White Guard*. He lived there during the Civil War. Afterwards the Soviets chopped it up into flats.'

'Yes,' Iain said. 'I said, I know.'

Simon stared ahead, down the winding slope. The river was somewhere below them but invisible in the darkness. He swallowed.

'So then,' Iain said. 'If we have any clue, about the bloody leak, we'll have to give it to them. You know, give them something – wolf from the door. I mean, if you know anything, or if you said anything—'

'Nothing, no. I just … I brought it in, Iain. I brought in the intelligence about the troops. One would have thought they'd be grateful. This wretched leak could have come from anyone – someone in the presidential administration, probably, trying to curry favour with the orange mob.'

'Right,' Iain said. 'Just, you know, they're spitting. Brent is. Top secret, he keeps saying. Not restricted, not confidential. Top fucking secret. And the girl, she's the same lass we had that little talk about, is she not? Anyway.'

'I've already told you everything I know. As I say.'

Simon looked up again from the road, lost his footing – that half-second of life-before-the-eyes, running-on-the-spot terror – but managed to steady himself.

'Careful,' Iain said. 'Good lad.'

'I am.'

They reached the bottom of the slope and headed across Podil, amid the pastel mansions, crumbling bas-reliefs and wrought-iron balconies; the mashed-up architecture of a bomb-haunted city. The vanguard picked up its pace on the flat ground. At Kontraktova Ploshcha they paused at the kerb to let a red and white streetcar pass, the heads inside lolling against the steamed-up windows, cushioned by their hats. An old woman sat on a fold-up chair outside the Metro, hawking pears, oranges and dill, her goods arrayed on a soggy newspaper in the slush at her feet. Another woman stood motionlessly in her rubber boots, holding bunches of wilting flowers in each hand, eyes fixed on the ground. Snow outlined the boughs of trees and the railings of balconies. Stray dogs nuzzled in the drifts that were banked around the rubbish bins.

Moored permanently alongside a bridge across the Dnipro, the restaurant boat was lit up like a carnival. The diplomats negotiated the boulevard that ran along the riverbank, scurrying between the cars in packs of two or three. Beyond the gangplank the staff wore tourist-board folk costumes, the waiters in Cossack pantaloons and silk sashes, the waitresses in embroidered blouses, garlands of flowers in their hair. The party was ushered up a flight of stairs and into an alcove in the prow of the motionless vessel, giving on to the main dining room. A band was tuning up.

They were twenty-one in total. The waiter who came for the order approached Iain instead of the ambassador; he turned towards her and she nodded. He asked for *salo*, borscht and black bread, plus *horilka* and *mors* to wash them down.

The liquor arrived and the toasting began – *To us! To international friendship! To freedom!* – the local habit they had all assimilated, a chance to simplify the world to sentimental parody, at least until the bottle was empty. Simon rose to toast the ambassador. Cynthia clinked glasses with Iain. She saw Simon watching her and smiled, then frowned, as if she were ashamed, disoriented, because she had smiled at her husband.

It was over. Not officially; officially they were still waiting for the Supreme Court to annul the election results. The tents were still pitched in the square and along Khreshchatyk, the marchers were still trudging up to the court and parliament and across to the electoral commission, flanked, still, by riot police and trailed by dwindling, disconsolate bands of counter-protesters. But after the troops were sent back to their barracks, the game was up. The next morning the opposition radio station had reported the bones of the debacle – the deployment, the American intervention, the countermanded order – information it attributed to a 'Western diplomat'. The Americans refused to comment, the presidential administration claimed the manoeuvre had been a training exercise, but everyone knew the regime was kaput. *Treason against the people!* Vlasych declared on the radio. *Mutiny of the patriots!*

It was over. There would be no bloodletting on Independence Square, just precautionary gunshots in *banyas* and convenient car wrecks meant to safeguard old secrets. There was an avalanche of defections by businessmen and ministers. The outcome the diplomats had coveted, even if they could not say so in public, was coming to pass: the bandits sent packing and the Kremlin with them. The right side would prevail – even if the Americans were spitting about the leak, up there in Kotsubinsky.

The band struck up a folk tune. Simon excused himself, dodging the waiters bringing up bowls of borscht and *vareniki* as he skipped down the stairs. As he doubled-back past the entrance, heading for the below-decks gents, Jacqui crossed the gangplank and arrived in the restaurant. They almost collided.

Her face was raw from the cold, her coat was open, she was out of breath, but behind her glasses her eyes were alight.

'Sorry,' Simon said. 'So sorry.'

'Sorry. Oh, it's you … Sorry.' She laughed, a true unguarded laugh. She pressed her glasses against her nose.

'We're upstairs.'

'Right-o.'

'I'm afraid you've missed the toasts.'

'Expect I'll survive.' She stepped aside for a couple arriving behind her. 'Don't you?'

'Are you … Is all well back at the ranch?'

'Yes, quite well, thank you,' Jacqui said, affecting a sardonic Regency tone. 'Feeding the beast, you know. They can't get enough of us at the moment, chasing up any old story.'

'You're a trooper.'

'Excuse me,' said a waiter bearing two platters of *shashlyk* at head height. Simon and Jacqui were shunted into the stairwell, beyond the glare of the lights.

'Well,' Simon said.

She cocked her head and regarded him quizzically. She did not speak. He coughed.

'Well,' he repeated, 'if I may, I—'

'Just' – she put a hand on his sleeve – 'just a moment.'

Simon glanced down at her hand; she left it there. 'What is it, Jacqui?'

In the shadows of the stairwell, her fingers on his arm, *horilka* riding through his veins, the encounter had the uncomfortable air of an assignation.

'It's just,' she said, 'I wanted to let you know, I was only away for a minute. Actually less than a minute, you must have come in at just the right moment. I mean the wrong one.' She spat out a chuckle.

'Jacqui,' he said, 'with the greatest respect, I don't have the faintest idea what you're talking about.'

She tightened her grip on his arm. 'The secure cupboard – I know it was you who reported it. The breach is on my record now, who knows what it'll cost me. But you knew that already.'

'I think – yes – Iain mentioned something like that, but I don't know the details, I'm afraid. Wasn't involved with that one. Minor matter though, shouldn't worry. Now, if I may …'

He placed his hand on top of hers and levered it off. She turned away from him and seemed to concentrate on the stairs, her mouth open roundly in a question.

'Right,' she said, 'well, it doesn't matter now.' She covered her eyes, murmuring to herself more than to Simon. 'Right thing to do in any case, the whole thing was getting out of hand.'

The ambassador's husband lurched past them, squiffily holding the banister on his way to the gents. 'Evening,' Simon said, pointlessly and too loud. He peered down into the well of the staircase. The boat was moving slightly, rocking, or he was.

Jacqui uncovered her eyes and straightened up. 'She was my contact, you know. Anyway.'

'Who was?'

'So really all of this should have been me.'

He rested the back of his hand against his brow like a soliloquising actor. 'Forgive me, Jacqui, it's late. I think we should discuss this another time.'

'If you say so.' She rolled her eyes. 'But – just – what I'm trying to say is, I've put too much into this. Much too much. I haven't seen my husband in three months, did you know that? Of course you didn't. I have to be a success here, I can't let ... I have to be.'

'And I have no doubt you will be.' The music filled the silence between them. 'Now, if you don't mind.'

He began to descend the steps to the lower deck. 'Some people,' she said loudly enough for him to hear, 'have it all their own way. So.'

Simon picked up his pace, cantering down the stairs, slowing up when he rounded the corner at the bottom and was out of her sight. He and the ambassador's husband squeezed past one another in the passageway. Jacqui climbed up to the dining room.

The dancing had begun. Iain had joined his younger colleagues on the dance floor, where he stood, immobile, drawing his splayed fingers in front of his eyes like veils, as if he were at a Glasgow nightclub in the seventies. The band had given up folk music in favour of Diana Ross and Beatles covers. Jacqui had taken a seat across the table from the ambassador. The food had barely been touched.

Simon stationed himself at the alcove's entrance. The lights of cars on the bridge shone through the window, pulses of red streaking over the water like tracer fire. He stroked his beard.

Cynthia had her back to him and did not see him approaching. He leaned on an adjacent seat, bent towards her and said, 'May I have the pleasure?' – much as he had at the wedding where they first met. He was obliged to repeat the suggestion at higher volume, almost shouting, to be heard above the band. His wife turned towards the question, her face close to his. She did not reply but rose from her chair and walked towards the music.

They did not touch. Others did, junior diplomats and diverse tipsy diners. Simon raised a hand towards Cynthia's hip but let it fall before he made contact. Instead they danced like thirteen-year-olds at a school disco, two feet apart, shuffling from side to side in semi-synchronicity, by the third number essaying simultaneous twirls. The knot of her silk scarf was drawn tightly around her neck but its tail floated as she spun, a hint of childhood ballet lessons in her deportment. Iain was now slumped on a stool beside the band, still drawing his fingers across his watery eyes.

It was over.

A flower-crowned waitress brought a platter of fruit but the diplomats ignored it. There was another bottle of *horilka* and some Armenian cognac. Jacqui sat alone at the table; the ambassador had left.

When the musicians took a break, Simon returned to the alcove to fetch his jacket and Cynthia's shawl. Jacqui called out to him. 'Dusting off the old moves?'

'Indeed.' He avoided eye contact, as people do when striving not to provoke the unhinged. 'Good suggestion by the boss, this outing. I think we all needed it.'

'Nice to see you and Mrs Davey having fun.'

Now he turned towards her. She removed her glasses, polishing them in her lap as she held his gaze with her short-sighted eyes.

'Thank you for your concern,' Simon said. Behind him the band struck up again, something by the Rolling Stones.

'Suppose we should all make the most if it. While we can.' She replaced her glasses.

A taxi was waiting to drive them up the icy hill. Simon tipped the cloakroom attendant and helped his wife into her coat. Outside, the clouds had cleared and the stars glowed. He paused on the gangplank; Cynthia hesitated beside him, and for a moment it seemed that they might kiss. Instead he offered his arm and escorted her to the car.

The driver took them on a circuitous route because of the encampment, ascending the slope to the Philharmonic and turning off at the museum. The floodlights above the stage beamed gaudily from Independence Square.

Together we are many!
We will not be defeated!

The car stopped in traffic on its way to the monastery and the plaza.

'Rather an enjoyable evening, don't you think? For everyone.'

'Yes,' Cynthia said. 'As a matter of fact, I do.'

She faced forwards, her eyes fixed on the driver's headrest.

Simon cleared his throat. 'And it looks as if we might be able to get home for the holidays after all. Depending on the rerun. Should know very soon.'

'So I gather,' Cynthia said. She coughed, as if correcting herself. 'Yes, that would really be very nice.'

Simon's hand crept across the taxi's back seat and clasped his wife's hand. She did not withdraw it.

vii. The magnolia tree

8.45 p.m.

THE ANTIQUE street lights are lit on the path between Kovrin's house and the river. The tide is low, the boats moored nearest to the bank perch nakedly on the brown muck. A woman is walking towards me, trailing a dog that seems too scruffy for the neighbourhood. I feel like a character in a science-fiction yarn who returns from another dimension, survives an alien abduction, and finds his old life obtusely unchanged. In that house, behind that wall, beyond the climbing roses – so I itch to tell the lady with the dog – right there, a cage is screwed into the basement. Beside it sits a guard named Timur with unaccountably kind eyes. Upstairs an impenitent billionaire is conducting a video conference. *Wake up!* I want to yell. *All of you, wake up!*

The woman has registered my disarray. Her eyes dart around and beyond me, searching for backup. She steps into the road and passes me without another glance, tugging the dog, viciously, when it hesitates to sniff my ankles. The dog whimpers and coughs. A pair of oarsmen are sculling on the river in the dusk, headlamps strapped to their foreheads, powerful and blithe. *Wake up!*

None of it would come as a surprise, I realise, to some of the people in this city – Kovrin and the cage, Timur and the shredded cup. Not to half the people in London, perhaps, nor to half the world. The surprisable half still live behind picket fences of the mind, in a fairyland of wilful, wanton innocence. A place in which politicians and their elections count for more than money. In which money is honestly come by – in which money has no smell, as Kovrin put it. The rest know that this city, this world, are host to every racket and heist that mortal imaginations can conjure. For them, surprise is dead, humankind has murdered it. Even if the faces change, they know, the rules stay the same, the principal one being that everything is for sale. Kleptocrats pose as revolutionaries. Pillars of the establishment twiddle their cufflinks and do the kleptocrats' bidding.

A pub nestles in the alleyway, and, notwithstanding my vows of abstinence, I slip in. Beamed ceiling, tobacco-stained panelling, leaded windows: the whole place is so authentic as to feel ersatz. The barmaid – Latvian, at a guess – pours me a glass of red wine. I find a seat at a small circular table with a view onto the water. A tabloid newspaper lies discarded on the companion stool, a pint-glass ring stencilled on the raucous front page.

He was only doing his job. David. Dylan. Damian. Dorian. That was it, Dorian – I met him once, I think, he came into the embassy. I am quite sure that is what he told himself. Much like the riot police and the snipers, and whoever poisoned the candidate and ruined his face. Kovrin's new man, Kovrin's old man. Doing their master's bidding: the scoundrel's alibi since the beginning of time. Just a job, to Dorian, to write those lies about me – or rather, one should acknowledge, lies plaited together with a strand of truth in such a way that, like the cleverest Russian *kompromat*, distinguishing between the two becomes impossible.

That in the hunt for the source of the leak, I was the prime suspect, and that a young local woman had been the conduit. He did not name Olesya, thankfully for her, but he described her with some precision, her height, her build, her complexion. That it appeared I had shared classified information with this woman – about the abortive crackdown on Independence Square, the Secretary of State's phone call, the wrangling – violating security protocols and compromising our alliances. How the Americans were livid. Spitting. Demanding that heads roll, pronto. Moreover, that I was known to have spent more time with this person than my professional duties required. Private time, intimate. *Déshabillé.*

In short, that we were believed to be having an affair, though by whom this was believed, he didn't specify. That I had a well-established weakness for young ladies – that, in fact, this was not my first indiscretion. Salivating at his keyboard when he came to that part, one could tell, though how he found out about it, God only knows.

How my marriage was believed to be wobbling. That I had a daughter.

First the Dorian character, and then, naturally, the rest of them. Fake news, one would call it these days. I would have survived the 'Western diplomat' stuff on the radio, the anonymous intel that, I now gather, Olesya yielded to Kovrin and he bartered for his mines. It was eminently plausible that someone else had blabbed: I believed as much myself, at first, or I tried to. But the story a few days later, naming me, was fatal. Deluded victim of the crudest honeytrap, that is how they portrayed me – look me up on the internet, in that museum of smears, and that is who I am.

They've already put it up, Iain told me on Independence Square.

I haven't the faintest idea what you're talking about.

It's too late, the story's already up. It's too late now.

I can't hear you, I can't hear what you're saying. Although I could.

I said, you've got to come with me. I warned you about her, did I not? Come on then.

Afterwards I didn't have the strength to sue. On reflection, what they wrote about our marriage was false and true at the same time. It was strained, of course, and yet, though I comfort myself with the notion that it was finished, dead on the inside if not in law, it wasn't entirely without hope. I think of that night – our last night, in a way, though at the time it seemed like a new start – the night at the floating restaurant. We danced. She smiled. In the taxi, we held hands. It was more than nothing.

A crew of men in boat-club polo shirts are leaving, heavy farewell slaps thudding off muscular backs, affection tamed by violence. I return to the bar and wait to be served. That night, on the Dnipro, that woman – Jacqui, the public affairs officer. Queer fish. But then, you never know what is happening in a colleague's life. Bereavement, divorce, nervous breakdown. A bloodcurdling medical test. In any person's life. Sometimes, in one's own.

She is an ambassador these days, if I recall correctly. Now it comes back to me: our woman in Minsk, I saw her on the news during the latest bout of protests there, smilingly reprimanding the government. Quite a poised performer. She came to the door of the embassy, I seem to remember, when they were packing us off to the airport.

Right, she said, as I ducked into the car. *Bon voyage.*

One never knows.

I call for another glass of Rioja and return to my table. Large glass again, I tell the Latvian. I congratulate myself for not slurping the wine before I sit down. Two large glasses equal most of a bottle, though one can pretend otherwise if the bottle remains behind the bar. This is the most I have drunk since descending to what, at the time, I took for my nadir. Waking up on the lavatory floor. Waking up on the pavement. No nights were spent in the cells during those lost months, but more than one constable advised that I move on – park bench, shop door. Soiling myself as I fumbled for my keys outside the flat.

Nancy read the report, of course. Damian's. Dorian's. No way to keep it from her. I imagine her in the common room of her house at school, sitting on one of their wicker chairs, scanning the computer screen, looking for the shape of her own name in the text, understanding that this time, unlike the last, our old life was definitively over.

That was a nuance old Dorian missed. One thinks back to the care one takes, when a child is young, to insulate her from that side of life. *Eros*, I mean. From that side of oneself. The giggly, cursing disengagements in the dark when a small hand pulls ajar the bedroom door. The quick flips onto my belly when she clambered into bed with us at dawn. And yet there I was, and there was she – Nancy – open-mouthed at the sight of my hand on another woman's rear, the woman's hand … An unknown quantity of seconds before we noticed her.

Simon, stop.

I don't want to stop.

Simon, I'm serious, stop it now. It's your—

What?

Daddy?

Her face went slack, as if she were comatose. As if she had been switched off and rebooted. She turned and ran.

You'd better go after her.

Come back … Popsicle, I'm sorry … Come back.

This was our family's primal scene – the moment behind the magnolia tree in Tel Aviv. Nancy was thirteen. I envisage her reliving it, three or four years on, as she read the guttersnipe's article, knowing all the allegations to be true, because she had seen the evidence for herself.

She is living in Milan, these days, so I glean from Facebook, working in an international school – she became a teacher in the end, she never did make it in the theatre. She didn't think to tell me she was moving abroad. Or she thought, but chose not to.

You're the best daddy in the world!

At the bar a posse of American tourists are discussing Stonehenge, loudly. I have an urge to rise from my stool, cross the carpet and shake them – that one, there, the man in the slacks with the pouch on his hip – hold him with my glittering eye and say: *Do not think that you are an exception. Do not believe that you will escape unscathed.* And after it happens, the divorce, the nightmare, the meltdown, do not expect to understand why. No celestial narrator will talk you through the story arc. What went wrong, when and why. You may not die alone but you will certainly die in ignorance.

The familiar warmth of the wine spreads across my chest and into my empty stomach. Yes, I took her into the box. That piquant detail didn't make it into the papers, but in the embassy they knew, albeit I was never told who saw us, and at the office in London. Improper, highly suggestive, but I cannot say that I regret it. The atoms that made up Olesya did so, temporarily, in the wrong room. She displaced the air in one place rather than another. In retrospect, that is what I should have said in my statement at the hearing: *Atoms out of place, old chaps.*

And yes, I talked too much. This was the high point of my professional life – I had played a part in history, such as few of us ever manage. Even now, that winter seems to me a pinnacle of idealism. People believed they could make a difference, that a difference could still be made, and they made one. I did. Or so we thought. In spite of everything, it is a happy memory, even if – as tends to be the case with summits, unless one exercises extreme caution – it led skiddingly to a headlong descent. For me, a sheer piste from triumph to disgrace. A swift disillusioning plunge for the other idealists, down into a swamp of 'paid everything', as Kovrin put it.

I flick over a cardboard beer mat lying on my table. The underside is stained but serviceable. Some people, in their cups, dial old flames, but my urge is always to write to my daughter. I go to the bar and ask the Latvian for a pen. She fishes a biro from her apron. *Dear Nancy* ...

My handwriting is crabby, the salutation squeezed into a beery corner to leave maximum room for my heart's disburdenment. Quickly I discover that I have only one thing to say.

I'm sorry. I ink the words several times, then cross them out. This, to put it mildly, has already been said.

I flip the mat back over and leave it on the table. I drain the dregs of my Rioja.

8. Together we are many

5 December

HE HEARD the commotion before he saw it. The sky was a cloudless field of blue, a pure midwinter blue that framed the Hotel Ukraina as Simon hurried down Mykhailivska Street from the embassy. At the bottom of the hill the glass-domed entrance of the shopping mall obstructed his view, but the frantic tooting of a horn – a baritone that suggested a lorry – pealed across Independence Square. It was the soundtrack of an emergency, but jollified by a harmony of chants and cheers, plus the distant backbeat of the steel drums.

Glory! Glory!

A text message beeped companionably in his inside pocket.

The crowd was packed in tightly around the edge of the stage, as dense as Simon had seen it, but its texture was different, the bodies yielding and relaxed as he weaved towards the road. Looking up towards the Lenin Museum he saw a truck inching through the horde, a group of protesters perched on its flat bed, arms aloft. Some of the drummers had detached themselves from the band in the park and were parading in the vehicle's wake. Somebody in the procession was speaking through a megaphone, a man, his face obscured by the flags and banners waving around him.

'This is your victory!' the megaphone man said. 'Glory to you all!'

Then a woman spoke. 'Dear friends!' she said, high-pitched but steely. 'Today, the world sees you! The people will never be defeated!'

As the truck reached the square, Simon made out the woman with the braid and the chocolatier. They hated one another, the whole city knew that, but they were on the same side, the side of truth against falsehood, the future facing down the past, the people versus the machine, which seemed, that afternoon, to be all that mattered. The rest was gossip.

'Dear friends,' the woman said, 'we have our election! We have a new election!'

A cheer rose from the square. People punched the air; people embraced. Next to Simon, a child asked her mother what was wrong, why was she crying? The woman with the braid relinquished the megaphone, not entirely voluntarily. 'The court has ruled,' the chocolate baron elaborated. 'The results are cancelled! Forward to victory!'

Glory!

In the vicinity of Simon's heart his BlackBerry beeped again. The temperature had risen a few degrees, a fleeting moderation that felt like a mercy. The snow that had accumulated in the side streets was softening into a grimy ooze. Still, it was only barely above zero; in a few weeks the river would start to freeze. He kept his coat zipped and his gloved hands in his pockets.

He turned and walked away from the hubbub, past the monument and towards the encampment on Khreshchatyk.

The police and security agents had melted away; it was as if, for a suspended, utopian moment, there were no authorities, there was no government, nor any need of them. Making his way towards the Conservatory to share the news with Olesya, he squinted at the roofs of the buildings that surrounded the square. No snipers were visible. Roadies of the revolution were setting out the microphones on the stage.

He saw Andriy first. Simon offered his hand but Andriy did not take it.

'Congratulations.'

'Is it?'

Two more beeps in his pocket. Simon's hand moved to his chest, resting there as if he were singing a national anthem.

Together we are many!

'You know, I'm sure you've heard, they've cancelled the results. The Supreme Court. There's going to be another election – same candidates, but much harder to falsify this time. Impossible, I'd say.'

'I know. And? You know Russians are here?'

'Where?' Simon said, scanning the square.

'Presidential administration. Bodyguards for president. You think they give up? Like this?' He clicked his gloved fingers noiselessly. 'Not so easy.'

'On the contrary,' Simon said. 'But I'm not sure what that lot can do about it now. The army has abandoned them, the crooks have been thrown off the electoral commission. Their best option is to go quietly.'

Andriy scowled. His cheeks were unshaven, his eyes blood-shot from sleeplessness. He was wearing his orange armband.

'Our struggle is not only here,' he said, rocking on his heels. 'Not only in Kiev. Watch also what happens in the east.

They say they will have their own vote, to make their own country. You hear this?'

'Yes, we've heard. We think it will die down. Not in anyone's interests. The territorial integrity – we have high confidence in the territorial integrity of your country. The Russians signed a treaty, they understand the limits.'

Andriy cleared his throat. 'Is nicer for you to think like this, I know. Cleaner. Happy ending, everybody go home. Peace and love. Problem is, we didn't pay.'

He hawked phlegm into his mouth as if to spit, but swallowed it instead. His Adam's apple throbbed in his throat.

'Excuse me?' More beeping in Simon's pocket.

Glory!

'We didn't pay enough,' Andriy said. 'We won this too cheap. For freedom you should pay, for any precious thing. For real freedom. No blood, so we never paid.'

He looked hard into Simon's eyes, which panned evasively beyond him to the crowd, the monument, the stage on which, having disembarked from the truck, the politicians were now mustering. In his hand Andriy clasped a flagpole, the flag itself rolled up so that the pole resembled a cosh. Simon smiled. Andriy did not reciprocate.

'This way is better,' Simon said, 'it must be. They're all switching sides now, you know. In parliament, the television stations. Kovrin's stations – have you seen the news? It's unrecognisable – now you're all heroes instead of terrorists. You can win without blood, Andriy. Not you *can*, you *have*. You've won.'

'For fifteen years we were independent,' said the woman with the braid, now speaking from the stage. 'And now we will be free!'

'We didn't pay,' Andriy repeated. 'So we win nothing.'

He gave a curt nod, turned and pressed roughly into the crowd. For a second, before the bodies closed behind him, a familiar figure materialised in the channel Andriy had opened, an apparition who seemed to be bending forward as if into the wind, leading with his moustache, coming the other way.

viii. The dog

IT IS FRESH on the river path now, a breeze rippling off the wine-dark water. The pointless hairs on my forearms stand to attention. The lights are on in the houseboats, the denizens of which always seem to me to have grasped a secret, something to do with freedom and priorities. A dog is straining towards me, towing its owner: same scruffy dog, same woman, now redder in the cheeks. The dog is concentrating, it wants to go home. The woman's eyes meet mine. Again she barrels past me, neck drawn in like an imperilled tortoise. This time the dog does not linger.

If you don't have a dog – how does the old Russian song put it? Let me see. *If you don't have a home, it can never burn down. If you don't have a wife, she can never betray you* (or, indeed, you her). *If you don't have a dog* – that's it – *your neighbour won't try to poison it.* Which do you choose? This is the question of the song. If you don't live, you will never need to die. To breathe is to gamble, as Kovrin maintained.

213

I poisoned the dog myself. That is the gruesome truth. Not Kovrin or Olesya or Dorian. My biography resembles one of those trick detective stories in which, after all the other suspects have been eliminated, it is clear that the narrator himself is the culprit. But I have the antidote in my hands. Quite literally, in my hands.

Do the good thing or do nothing.

A disco boat screeches past in the middle of the river. Three geese have hopped onto the wall, beside a forgotten champagne glass. There are salmon in there now, they say. When people leap from the bridges, I recall reading, the strong, submerged currents can whisk them downstream, deep down in the murk, so that they pop up, dead and drowned, miles to the east, towards the sea.

I walk across the grass in the small park to a rowan tree in the corner, close to a high garden wall, hang my bag on a silvery branch and slip off my shoes. No one appears to be watching. Removing my trousers and underpants, I put on my inelegant, checked bathing costume. I stuff my clothes into the bag, shoes on top, wallet, phone and keys inside them. Olesya's email address remains in my pocket, a clue they might use to put me back together, should anyone be inclined to. Between her and me, only one of us deserves the punishment I contemplated on the platform this afternoon.

Somehow I expect a response from the world when I step out from behind the tree – alarm or perhaps amusement – but the world declines to notice my modest paunch and rounding driver's shoulders. Two joggers, an exponent of tai chi, a man with a ponytail strumming a guitar for three women at a liquid picnic: nobody comments. No one calls the police. As I approach the river I notice a tattoo on the nape of the tai chi lady's neck. It puts me in mind of Polly's neck, Polly's tattoo, Olesya's Polly, which I spotted after she changed into her dress. It occurs to me that the Latvian barmaid and Timur, the henchman with the kind eyes, may be the last human beings with whom I converse in this life. I smile a little and quicken my pace.

Tiddly-pom, my mother would have called my condition. Not drunk, not really. Tipsy. I stroll onto the pier, up and over to the jetty, arms crossed in front of me against the mild chill. I reach the ladder that descends into the soup. What a long, long day this has been.

I do not plunge into those swirling currents. I do not jump. I lower myself down the rungs sedately. The water is not as cold as one might have anticipated – less mortifying than the temperature I am accustomed to in the park – but it is dark and viscous, adhering somehow to my skin. Tendrils or tentacles ghost around my ankles. At knee depth I glance into the window of the nearest houseboat, the *Queen Bess*. A girl, a young woman, is playing an upright piano, an older woman listening from a narrow sofa. I cannot make out the music.

Down I go, and out from the shallows. The current finds me as I make for the middle. Preposterous, really, the details one's brain retains, the mnemonic bandwidth occupied by errant trivia, even as vital knowledge goes astray. As I breast-stroke against the current's pull, I think of an instant at a picnic fifty years ago. My beard is sodden and cold. We were in a field, a wheat field, a blanket spread out on the verge, and my father stoops to pick something up – I cannot now think what it was, an item of cutlery, or a handkerchief, or a cricket ball. I know that he bends at the waist, a palm at the small of his back, and as he bends the sun is sitting beyond him at such an angle, the smile on his face is so unguarded, so unwonted, that it sticks with me and comes back to me now. Perhaps that is not strange after all.

The water becomes heavier and denser. The wine dulls the pain in my shoulder from the bodyguard's ministrations, but inevitably my arms tire. Another riverine factoid that I now recall: in Paris, in the nineteenth century, they could always tell, when they dredged out the suicides from the Seine, which of them were spurned lovers and which were debtors. The lovers had scratches of paint beneath their fingernails, signs of an edge-of-the-parapet change of heart, whereas the debtors sank like stones.

I am not altogether sure which category I belong to. Both, maybe. Errors of judgement and unrequited love.

Ahead of me a gash of neon runs horizontally along the bridge. Somewhere a foghorn sounds. This far out the water is choppier, my body is numbing, my breath rasps. Spreading my limbs as if I were an insect, I begin to let the current take me, down to the bottom, out to sea. I close my eyes against the splashes, like a child.

A child in a swimming pool in America, say, doggy-paddling in her purple bathing suit. *You can do it, popsicle! It's better to try*, Olesya said today in her crowded digs. Evidently she herself is still trying, in spite of everything. *Eat the kasha*, Kovrin told me in his mansion. *Adapt.*

It's better to try.

No, I realise, righting myself in the river at what must be almost my last opportunity. Enough of what I used to be abides. No. Not tonight. Not like this.

I describe an ungainly circle and head back towards the bank, face down, hurrying, turning my head to spit out the slimy water. I have come a shorter distance than I had thought, but the way back seems interminable. My hurt arm throbs. Sober now, I make for the *Queen Bess* but fall short, emerging onto the sludge below the river wall, sinking up to my ankles, my shins. A family of sandpipers glance at me and wade on.

My fingers clutch a ladder at the end of the houseboat. Halfway up, I peep through the window. The girl is still playing the piano. This time she sees me and waves.

I haul myself out and gasp across the gangplank. Two joggers arc around me, like rivulets around a rock, as I stand on the path, dripping. As I head back across the lawn I find that my bag is still hanging from the tree. I can see the heel of a shoe protruding among the branches. Buried below it is Olesya's note. Perhaps, on reflection, I will ask her to write to Nancy for me.

Reaching in the bag for my towel, it seems almost as if I had never been in the river at all. I shiver.

9. Will not be defeated

5 December

OLESYA WAS sitting astride a young man's shoulders, a man Simon had not met before, dancing with her arms as the music played between speeches. Her head was thrown back, her white neck exposed above the collar of her thin black coat.

Beep. His hand was at his zip when she looked down and saw him. She waved and toppled, the unknown man stooping to allow her to leap off. She grabbed Simon's forearms to cushion her fall, kept her footing and laughed to find herself upright. Alive, on Independence Square, and safe.

'Thank you. I may break my neck.'

'On the contrary,' Simon said. 'Thank *you*.'

'Is it true?'

'Yes, there'll be a new election, in a few weeks, apparently.'

'It means that this – all this – we really did something.'

'Some of you more than others.' *Beep.* 'You know, Olesya – I wanted to tell you – the other night, what might have happened here doesn't bear thinking about. What I mean is, it's partly down to you that ... What is it?'

Her expression had clouded, as if the news on the square were dire rather than euphoric. 'I must say, what they reported on the radio, I myself never spoke to—'

'You don't have to say. I expect it came from someone in the administration, some disgruntled apparatchik or other. No harm done.'

'Please listen —'

'It's okay, Olesya, really. I trust you.'

For a few seconds she turned away. A patriotic ballad blared from the sound system. Simon caught sight of Yaryna, bouncing on another man's shoulders, her earmuffs jiggling to the beat; he waved but she didn't notice him

'It's strange,' Olesya said. 'All these people here, and only two ... Only we two ... Only we ...'

'Yes,' he said. 'But, you know, when a person – two people – between two people ... What I'm trying to say is, between two people something can happen, and even if no one else knows about it, it still happened, it's still real. Do you follow me? Like the tree in the forest that falls and no one hears – the tree fell all the same. What you and I did together, we'll always have it, no matter what.'

'It's clear. It means it's for ever, whatever will be.'

Simon began to reach for her hand, but the alerts in his pocket became too frenetic to ignore. He unzipped his coat and fished inside for the BlackBerry; it throbbed in his palm like an animal in spasm. He removed a glove, entered his password and scanned the screen. Nine texts in the last hour, corresponding to those nagging beeps. He rolled and clicked to his emails. Twelve since he left his office. Thirteen. Fourteen, the new messages stacking on top of one another as he watched. Three missed calls from the embassy, two from Cynthia, one from a London number he didn't recognise. *Nancy. Something's happened to Nancy.*

He dialled voicemail and raised the phone to his ear but could not hear the message in the melee. Instead he opened the ambassador's most recent email; as the words appeared on the screen, the poisoned candidate took to the stage, his hands outstretched and waving, a giant orange scarf wreathed around his shoulders. Simon stilled his thumb.

'Dear friends,' the candidate said. 'This is your victory!'

Glory!

'Glory!' Olesya chanted. She passed her arm through Simon's and levered him towards her. In his pink fingers the BlackBerry beeped unrelentingly.

'Glory to you all!' proclaimed the president-in-waiting. 'Your glory will never die!'

The man's wife appeared at his side. He steepled his hands and raised them aloft for his peroration. 'Onwards to Europe! Onwards to freedom!'

The office called, the ambassador's email said. *They called twice. It is imperative that we respond today. Now.*

It didn't sound as though it was anything to do with Nancy. *Thank God.*

The anthem of the revolution boomed across the square. Olesya steered Simon into a patch of space, pivoted to face him and took his hand. They danced, he clumsily, bending his knees but not moving from the spot as she stepped towards him and out again. Around them, people were clapping to the beat and singing. Olesya laughed and Simon laughed too, the exultation of a moment that could never be surpassed or cancelled. The pouches around her eyes seemed to have cleared.

He felt a touch on his collar and, still holding Olesya's hand, turned to look behind him. There was Iain, not smiling, though Simon still was, because after all they were celebrating, something good and indelible had happened in the stubborn world.

Seizing him by both shoulders, Iain rotated Simon's torso. He was obliged to release Olesya; Iain's face appeared before him instead, his rheumy, regretful eyes and walrus moustache. He leaned forward to whisper into Simon's ear.

A note on names

Purely for reasons of familiarity, *Independence Square* spells 'Kiev' this way, rather than 'Kyiv', which is how the capital city is properly transliterated from Ukrainian.

The name of a character in this book was chosen by the winner of an auction held by the National Literacy Trust. The trust is a British charity that works to improve literacy in disadvantaged communities.

KIEV

SCALE
(metres)
0 — 500

KONTRAKTOVA PODIL
PLOSHCHA

PETRO SAHAIDACHNY ST.

ANDRIYIVSKY DESCENT

St. Andrew's
Church

Ministry
of Foreign
Affairs

DESYATYNNA ST.

British
Embassy

Princess Olga
monument

St. Michael's
Monastery

MYKHAILIVSKA ST.

VELYKA ZHYTOMYRSKA STREET

Bohdan Khmelnytsky
monument

St. Sophia's
Cathedral

OLD KIEV

SOFIIVSKA ST.

YAROSLAVIV VAL STREET

VOLODYMYRSKA STREET

INDEPENDE
SQUARE

Central
Post Office

Tchaikovsk
National Mus
Academ

BOHDAN KHMELNYTSKY STREET

National Opera
of Ukraine

KHRESHCHATYK STREET

SHEVCHENKO BOULEVARD

FOMIN
BOTANICAL GARDEN

Besarabsky
Market

Site of
Lenin statue

SHEVCHENKO
PARK

BASEINA ST.